CHASING *Wildfire*

J. LUM

Chasing Wildfire—Version 1

Copyright © 2019 J. Lum

ISBN **(e)** 978-0-9991423-4-9

ISBN **(p)** 978-0-9991423-5-6

Editing—Jenn Wood with All About The Edits

Cover Design—Marisa Rose-Shor of Cover Me Darling LLC

Image copyright © 2019

Photographer—Eric Battershell

Cover Model—Chris Williamson

Formatting—T.E. Black Designs; www.teblackdesigns.com

“Cause all that you are is all that I'll ever need”
— ED SHEERAN, *TENERIFE SEA*

*To my Wonder Pug Lani, you gave me almost twelve years of love and
all that puggy goodness. I love you.*

This is never goodbye, but see you later.

prologue

BEN

I HATE TIES. *HATE, HATE, hate.* I know, hate is a strong word. My Ma, who was a Catholic loving sort of woman, used to tell me, "hate is not to be used in my household." That it tempted the devil. I guess I will go with *loathe* then. Can't tempt anyone with that one. So, Father John can kiss it.

Now here I am, in the nicest office in downtown New York City. I drove up from Lancaster to hang out with Toby, who's been my roommate at Harvard the last few years. My Ma wanted me help down at the mills, but I couldn't handle grinding down trees the whole summer. I've always had an open invite from the Cardonas, so this time, I took it.

I wanted to see more than the rural lands and buggies. Attending one of the most prestigious universities in the world on a full-ride scholarship was going to get me out. I could set Ma up so she didn't have to work the two jobs she always has, just so she could put food on the table. My deadbeat dad was no use. He took off on us a long time ago, and sending Ma fifty here and there wasn't enough for our family.

I met Toby freshman year. Immediately, I recognized we were like oil and vinegar, but when mixed, we made the perfect combination. Toby likes to say I'm "blue-collared" to all our buddies. To the average nobody, that would be an insult, but Toby means it as a compliment. I was the student on a full ride, who knew how to work with my hands and make a dollar, while he was the spoiled kid from Cali, with a rich father. Deep down inside, I think he envied me while I envied him.

Despite the major differences, we took to each other pretty well. I'm the more serious of the two. He spends most of his time chasing tail while I have my head in the books. I don't have a choice—I need to keep my grades up to continue receiving the scholarship money since my Ma can't afford the tuition. She couldn't even afford to send me to state college, even if she tried. I have four other siblings, and my loser father certainly wasn't going to help.

So, my nose is either in a book or at the local pub, helping with security. It's the busiest pub downtown, it's classy, and I make good money on the nights I work the door. I could be making more as a bartender, but I'm only twenty and "Uncle Charlie" can't afford to lose his liquor license over a family friend's kid. I'm not the biggest guy, but he's seen me take on a few Southies who would get out of hand. I earned my respect from Uncle Charlie and the rest of the crew.

Case in point, just before going home for the summer, one of Uncle Charlie's regulars got handsy with one of the girls drinking. He was a big, burly dude, not at all inconspicuous, and must've been knee-deep in some whisky when things got out of hand. I knew which crew he was with and they had a "no touch" rule, so I knew something was up. The guy who runs the crew doesn't take kindly to any of his men being out of hand with any lady. Crazy but true. I've heard stories of him breaking hands of guys who got fresh with one of the local girls.

The shiner that's slowly fading right now is from the one punch he got in after I pulled him off the girl. Me and one of Uncle Charlie's guys managed to straighten him out, and all without calling the cops. Uncle Charlie handed me a wad of cash and thanked me for stopping the guy. I tried to give it back since that was the job he had me doing, but he didn't want it back. Said to keep it, since I needed it for that *big, fancy school* I was attending.

"Mr. Dunn. Mr. Cardona is ready to see you now. He apologizes, the phone call to London took much longer than he thought." The woman who introduced herself as Jenn earlier is hovering, smirking down at me. Probably laughing on the inside, at my attempts to straighten this tie for the thousandth time. I'm already fidgety and nervous as hell.

Before she gets too far away from me, I gently tap her shoulder. "Thanks for helping me find my way around earlier, but before I go in, do you know why he's asked to see me? Toby refused to tell me. He just said that I was to come here while he ran an errand, and that I had to wear a suit."

She turns to face me, smiling. "I'm not sure. He just said to set aside some time between his phone calls." Then she winks. "But really, you don't need to be nervous. Mr. Cardona is really nice." She knocks on the door and pats me on the shoulder.

"Come in." I walk through the doors and immediately, the view of downtown New York sits before me. The office is covered in floor-to-ceiling windows. To say this office is pure luxury would be an understatement.

"You can come on in, Benji." I cringe when I hear my full name. Only my Ma calls me Benji, and Toby when he wants to be crass with me.

"Hi, Mr. Cardona." I walk further into his office as he stands from his nice mahogany desk, and shake his hand. His office is warm and inviting, nothing like what I expected a Fortune 500 company executive office to look like. His expansive desk looks lived in, and he has a conference-like table off in the corner. What is more prominent are the comfy-looking chairs and couches in front of his desk.

"Please, call me Sebastián. Come sit down, I'm sure you're wondering why I had Toby ask you to come to my office." With a hearty laugh, he gestures towards one of the plush chairs I'd been admiring.

I adjust my tie again. I know it's from being nervous. I don't like not knowing things, and having Mr. Cardona ask me to come here with no idea why puts me on edge. I've met him plenty of times over the last few years. He and Mrs. Cardona have been more than generous with me when they've come down to visit us. I don't know how much Toby has mentioned to them about my finances, but my suspicions are they know a lot, especially since they'd always come with a handful of supplies, and the refrigerator and cabinets were never empty. I was the poor kid rooming with their son the last few years.

"So, I heard from Toby you're the top student this past year? Congratulations. That was no small feat, tackling Applied Sciences and Economics." He leans back in his chair and looks at me, as if accessing me for a job or recruitment. Surely, he wouldn't be looking to bring me on board, I haven't even graduated.

"I've always been good with numbers and computers.

Toby is a lot smarter than me though." I shrug, unsure what else to say, other than, "Sure, you're right."

He throws his head back in a hard laugh. "Don't be too modest with me, Benji. You and I both know my son doesn't have the drive like you do. I know he chases girls more than he puts his head in books. I talked to a few of your professors there. Your advisor in the Economics Department is an old college buddy of mine. He spoke highly of you the last time I was up in Boston." I swallow hard, my mouth drier than normal. I'm a little speechless since Toby never mentioned his father knew my advisor.

"Sorry, I didn't mean make you uncomfortable." He leans a little forward and pushes the unopened water bottle sitting on the table closer to me.

"I'm not uncomfortable." I shift a bit and reach out to uncap the water.

"Benji, I've seen you get nervous before." He chuckles lightly while giving me a minute to compose myself. Grabbing the bottle, I take a big swallow of the cold water. "Plus, you're clenching and unclenching that left hand of yours. You and Toby do the same thing when you're nervous or upset."

I quickly look down at my hand and unclench. When I look back up to his face, his eyes are alight and he looks slightly amused at my discomfort.

"Sorry, just a bit nervous, and this tie is feeling a tad too tight." I adjust it again, loosening the middle. I know I should be more professional; Toby had mentioned to me his dad was a stickler for proper attire in the workplace.

"You can take the tie off if it's bothering you so much. Not sure why you decided to dress so nicely." He shifts a bit in his seat and grabs a cup of coffee off the table.

"Toby said…" I blurt.

"Toby told you that I asked you to dress up. And you

believed him." He rubs at his eyes as he continues to laugh at my expense, before he grows serious. "So, jokes aside, while talking to Professor Aldridge, he mentioned that the University of Edinburgh next year will be having a few important visiting professors teaching at the business school there."

I groan because Professor Aldridge had been needling me all year about this study abroad program. I'm on a four-year academic scholarship, but it barely covers my tuition and housing expenses. My job at the pub is for the essentials and maybe a little money to my Ma and family back home.

"He mentioned it a few times." I pick at the label on the bottle, not sure what else to say. I would love to attend there for the semester. Harvard, unfortunately, doesn't have a business school for undergrad, but I get the added benefit of being able to double major in Applied Sciences and Economics, which will include heavy statistics and computer skills.

In other words, it's a guaranteed job after I graduate.

A study abroad program that snags two renowned business professors, who also specialize in Theoretical Economics, while also hosting a tenured professor in International Business and Law would be a dream, but I just can't afford it.

"And…?" I look up to see Mr. Cardona smirking at me again. I had told Professor Aldridge I just couldn't make it work, without going into too much detail. I need the job I have to get me through the rest of the year. Uncle Charlie would hire me back but what do I do while abroad? I couldn't exactly pick up a job. I was stupid enough to look it up—if I got caught working on the down low, that could cost me a lot, and I'm pretty sure I could potentially lose my academic scholarship. Harvard wouldn't look kindly to a rule breaker.

"I just can't make it work, as much as I would like to do the study abroad program. The scholarship wouldn't cover all my expenses over there." I didn't want to lie, and he didn't know the whole deal.

"What happens if that wasn't a problem?" He smirks at me again before taking another sip of his coffee.

"I don't take handouts, I'm not a charity case. And always pay my own way," I bit out, my tone clipped. I don't mean to be rude, but that question puts my hackles up. I don't want to owe anyone. Ever. Owing anyone anything always comes back to bite you, I learned that early in life. I watched my mom, thinking she "owed" my father, like it was some duty. All it did was ruin her.

"I appreciate the candor, Benji, but if you don't mind taking a bit of advice from this old man. Not everything in life is a handout. I know what it means to struggle for every dollar." He pauses and looks out the window, like he's watching something. "I didn't always have this." He gestures around the room. "I've been where you're at. So, it isn't a handout to want to help. To ask for help. It doesn't take anything away from you. Doesn't make you less of a man either."

"But…"

"I understand the 'but.' The 'but' should be, I see a lot of potential in you. Toby said you're the smartest guy on campus. I take what my son tells as the honest truth. He's a good judge of people. I also believe that, after talking to your advisor. I also know you're working at that pub downtown, trying to make ends meet. This is an opportunity *I* don't want you to miss."

His piercing eyes stare back at me. "What would you say if I was looking to hire you on here at Cardona Financial after you graduate?"

"I would say you were nuts. I've never…I'm not even a business major. I wouldn't even know…" I blurt out.

Mr. Cardona bursts out laughing. "I'll let you on a secret, Benji. No degree will teach you everything. You've got two more years before graduating Harvard, before you're virtually pushed out in the real world. Book smarts is good, it's applicable. But where you'll learn everything is in-house. You've got two years under me, to learn if you want."

His eyes twinkle, like he knows he's pulled me in. "You'll be on a paid internship during the summers. I can get you into your own housing, but I think Toby and you rooming in our home works out, if you're comfortable. Mrs. Cardona is happy to have you stay with us. But the kicker is, you will have to attend that study abroad program. I won't budge on that."

"I don't get it. Why me?" He's thrown me for a loop. A guaranteed job, and two years to learn valuable skills under a man who built a company from the ground up. A company that's had accolades for the last handful of years. It's all too good to be true.

He smirks again at me, as if I've just asked the dumbest question in the world. I'm just some poor kid from Lancaster who knows nothing. "What's not to get? I've known you for years. You're smart, quick on your feet, and honest to a T. And you work hard. Those are skills you don't necessarily learn, but are inherent. Values I see as being important in this world. To my world.

"People come here because they trust us with helping them make informed financial decisions. We are not talking a few thousand dollars here and there, Benji. Millions, and sometimes *billions*, of dollar-type decisions. I need people I can trust. I'm not getting younger. I won't be at Cardona Financial forever. Someday soon, I'd like to pass this on to

Toby and Jamie since they've both shown interest. That means fresh blood coming into a business I love and care for. I want my people taken care of."

It's hard to resist a speech like that. Working and learning under Sebastián Cardona would be something incredible.

"I don't know what to say." I'm honestly left speechless. It's a lot to take in. I never expected I would be offered a job when I came up here.

"You can say yes. I'm not going to be easy on Toby, or you. It's a lot of responsibility that I will be putting on both of you. I know this. Jamie is still too young. Every mistake you make can mean the ruin of another person or company, so keep that in mind," he says in a serious tone.

"How long do you expect me to work for Cardona Financial?"

"You're wondering what the catch is, aren't you?" I nod my head, the skeptic in me making an appearance, because I'd rather know upfront, before committing to anything permanent. Shoot, he could ask me stay in a job I hate for years. As good as the offer sounds, I won't lock myself down forever.

"I only ask the best from you. To keep studying hard, learn everything you can while in Scotland, and at Harvard. I want to expand Cardona Financial globally in the next few years, so getting as much experiences in international business is important to me. That means being comfortable abroad."

"I don't know if I can make that commitment now, when I'm not one hundred percent positive what I want to do. Plus, like you said earlier, not everything is book smarts. What if I make a mistake?" I fidget in my seat and take another big gulp of water. He's being candid and honest with me, so I reciprocate. What he's asking of me is a heavy expectation I don't know if I can fulfill.

"I think you'll stay on because you enjoy what Cardona Financial can offer you. I believe you'll work hard to make the right decisions. I'm not just going to throw you to the wolves. Me and my other executives will be there to help. I think you can benefit and apply what you learn when you work with us full-time after graduation. In short term, I believe in you. If you decide to not stay on after graduation, I won't have hurt feeling if you decide to go somewhere else. I want what's best for you, Benji, I always will."

Mr. Cardona pauses to take a few deep breaths. "But don't think I won't try to guilt you into staying." He laughs mirthlessly. "Not illegally, of course, but I will help convince you that Cardona Financial is the right choice in the end."

He mentioned the study abroad program as a deal breaker. I think back to all the requirements and details, and realize I may be too late. I cringe, thinking all this conversation would be for nothing.

"If you're thinking deadlines, you aren't late to apply. Professor Aldridge already made a phone call on your behalf, and they are holding that slot for you. Don't worry about the financials, Benji, they'll all be covered by me personally."

"How did you know?"

"How'd I know that you were thinking about it? I know everything, Benji, just remember that."

I shake my head because now I think he's pulling my leg. Mr. Cardona and I talked some more about what was going to be expected of me. He even took me around the office, introducing me to all of his top executives, each of them telling me a little about their background. All diverse and versatile.

I slowly start to understand why Cardona Financial is

successful. Sebastián Cardona believes in versatility in the workforce and utilizes each of his employee's strengths to build a company that understands the needs of others.

After spending the afternoon with him, I realize he was right. He had an uncanny way of convincing me the right decision was to say yes. To show me I could belong here despite everything. Despite my fears, I'm up for a challenge and it excites me to see where this opportunity could take me.

Thank you, unnecessary tie.

CHAPTER one

BEN

I'VE NEVER TRAVELED OUTSIDE OF the United States. Shoot, I've never traveled anywhere past the East Coast, so flying across the ocean to study under some of the most prestigious professors in Europe is something I never dreamed could ever happen to me.

Since I'd said yes to Mr. Cardona's proposal, everything has been a whirlwind. Toby had been grinning like a Cheshire cat when his dad and I had left to go back to the house. Taking one look at his face, I knew the jerk had known everything his dad had planned, and still gave me no insight. As much as I wanted to rail on him for keeping that a secret, I also appreciated his enthusiasm. He talked on and on about how cool it was going to be working together. I'd been so busy getting the best grades that I could get, I didn't have time to think that our lives were going to change after college. Now, we had a chance to continue to work together. That in itself was comforting.

The next day, I'd been shuffled into Human Resources and spent the better part of the early morning signing a bunch of paperwork, so I could start my benefits. I know Mr. Cardona said it would be a paid internship but he never mentioned I'd get full benefits, which included a business phone I could keep even while in school, but Cardona Financial would also be giving me a stipend while at Harvard, and covering my health insurance. When I started at Harvard, as a student, I was required to have some type of medical, but it was shitty state insurance.

Ma cried for an hour when I told her what the Cardonas were doing for me. She even made me hand the phone over to Mr. and Mrs. Cardona, so she could thank them personally. When I'd gotten into Harvard, it was a dream of hers that I could get out of Lancaster and make something of myself. She believed higher education would give our family a fighting chance. My sisters and I wouldn't become another failed lower-class statistic.

What floored me even more was what happened once everything was final. Mr. Cardona had taken me under his wing, along with Toby. We were in every single meeting that summer, learning about all the accounts he'd been overlooking. We even got to handle a few of the smaller accounts with supervision, and by the end of the summer, I'd learn the ropes of how the business functioned. I even got to help write up a plan Cardona Financial could benefit from if it made some modifications. The executives and Mr. Cardona were impressed with our assessment. The plans were passed on to my advisor, who was able to place that on my college records as successfully completing an internship, something Harvard expected of us.

The expenses for Scotland were fully covered, and Mr. Cardona handed me an international bank card, instructing me to use it at my discretion. I vowed to use it as little as possible. The housing and tuition were covered, so I didn't need much. I was told to "just learn and to enjoy myself."

Mr. and Mrs. Cardona made sure my whole trip over was comfortable, though the first-class seats seem to be overdoing things. I would've been happy to sit in coach, but they wouldn't hear of it. I wish Toby could've come, but his grades wouldn't have been enough to get him into the program.

"Sir… Sir… Please wake up." I feel someone nudging my shoulder and a bright light hits my eyes. "Sir, we're going to start our pre-landing procedures. You need to get up and put your seat up in the upright position."

"Ohh, okay. Thank you." I rub at my eyes and feel for the button to put my sleeper seat back up.

"You're very welcome. Would you like anything to drink before we land?" I blink and see the nice flight attendant who'd been very attentive during our flight over.

"Umm… can I get a Coke with no ice, please?" I finally get the seat to the upright position and snap my seat belt into place.

"Of course, I'll be right back."

"Thanks, umm… How long until we land?"

"About thirty minutes, sir." The nice lady walks off, and I look around the cabin and see the people around me opening up their window blinds. I follow suit, so I can see the view. We're dropping altitude and now I can see everything below.

Prior to the trip, I read Scotland's weather could be fickle. True to her word, we are pushing past murky clouds and it looks like it's about to rain. But past the bad weather, I can see open land for miles. Rolling hills of green and purple lighting our trip to Edinburgh. The Cardonas arranged for me to arrive a little early, allowing me settle into Edinburgh before school starts.

When we finally land, I turn on my phone as soon as I'm allowed. The phone pings like crazy.

Toby: *Hey fucker, enjoy yourself!*

Mr. Cardona: *Let Mrs. Cardona and I know when you arrive safely. Have fun! Use the card! It's not just for emergencies.*

Toby: *Make sure and tell me if you find some hotties. 😉 I can live vicariously thru you. European chicks = H-A-W-T*

Mrs. Cardona: *Sebastián forgot to tell you. There will be a driver waiting for you. Don't take a taxi. He has your number so he might call if he can't find you! X Debi. P.S. Don't forget to call your mother!*

Toby: *Hey, Debi wanted to make sure you don't take a cab. Call your Ma too. Oh, and Dad said make sure you use the card whenever you want! Don't be a stubborn mule…*

Unknown Caller: *Hello, Mr. Cardona arranged for me to pick you up and take you over to the university. Please call or text me back when you arrive in baggage. I will be awaiting with a sign that says 'Mr. Dunn' on it.*

Toby: *Dad said he emailed you a list of*

*contacts over there too if you need it.
Bring me a bottle of whiskey back. 20 = old
enough to drink!!*

***Ma:** Please call me when you land. Worried.
Love you, Benji! The girls say hi and take
lots of pictures.*

GOOD GRACIOUS, I HAVEN'T EVEN HAD A CHANCE TO LAND before they bombarded my phone. I quickly text back the unknown caller that I've landed before collecting my carry-on items and stepping off the plane, into a new adventure and a new opportunity.

Customs was uneventful, thankfully, and I make my way out to find the driver. As I get closer to the doors, I see a line of men in suits holding signs, and smile when I see a man in a bowler hat and tweed coat holding a sign with my name on it. He smiles back as I make my way to him.

"Mr. Dunn? I'm Calum. Is this all ye have for baggage?" He eyes the lonely checked bag and my carry-on. "Mrs. Cardona mentioned you'd be attending the university. Seems low on baggage." He chuckles as he grabs both bags.

"Oh, I can get those." I try to reach for the larger of the bags.

"Ah lad, I got yer bags. Just follow me this way." I walk alongside quietly as I look around. The airport looks fairly small, much smaller than JFK and Logan.

"Is it always this dreary?" I can't believe I'm asking this man about the weather, but the silence is killing me.

"Aye, it's *dreich* today. I wish you'd see my country with better weather, but it'll be like this all afternoon." He tips his hat to one of the men we passed as we make our way to his car. "Here we are, please settle in. I'll get yer bags stowed." He grabs the small carry-on to place in the trunk.

"Do you mind if I sit up front with you?" I gesture.

"O'course, keep this old man company! First time in Edinburgh?" I listen carefully to what he's saying—his accent is thick with Scottish brogue. A few words are a little harder to understand, but I'm getting the gist. The way he says Edinburgh is so much different than what I would've thought it was pronounced.

"Yes, sir. It's my first time ever out of the United States." I smile as he comes around to the driver's side. I don't think I'll be able to get used to sitting on the opposite side.

"Excellent. So, Mr. Cardona mentioned he wanted me to take ye the scenic route. So ye can get the feel of the city. If ye want to stop anywhere, we can. I'll be available for the next few days." He smiles broadly.

"What?" Toby's dad made no mention of me having a driver while here in Edinburgh. I quickly grab my phone and sent a text to Toby.

"Aye, lad. Yer Da didnae want ye to travel alone the first few days. He said he wished he was able to drop ye off himself, but he was stuck in some important meetings." He pulls up slowly to the parking service guy and they chat for a second before he tips his hat to him.

"He's not my dad. Family friend and, well, I guess, boss," I quickly mutter.

"Oh sorry, Mr. Cardona gave me the impression he was your Da. Well, lad, this is Edinburgh. I'll be drivin' ye around the old part of the city and up 'round the Royal Mile. I can park and we can walk up towards the castle." He's got his eyes on the road, but by the inflection of his voice, I can tell how proud he is of his country.

"So, have you lived in Edinburgh your whole life?" I wince because I know I totally butchered saying Edinburgh.

"Ahhh, you'll get used to it, lad." He joyfully laughs as he winds around a circular part of the road. I grab hold of the door as I watch several cars ringing about. "Roundabout."

"What?" I grip the door handle a little tighter as I watch a car drive by, really close to another car.

"That's a roundabout. Do ye not have roundabouts in America?"

Laughing, I loosen my grip around the door. "Not like that, and I don't know how you are driving on that side of the road. I would totally hit a car."

"Well, when you've been driving as much as I have, lad, ye get the hang of things. For ye, I wouldn't drive around Edinburgh. It's too much traffic." He swings a left. "So, where's about America are you from?"

"Born and raised in Pennsylvania, but I attend college in Cambridge." We are moving quick fairly down what looks like a main road, and so far, the view is unremarkable. Lots of green and every once in a while, houses and buildings pop up. Scotland, so far, reminds me of home.

"Cambridge, ah, just like England. This is Glasgow Road. We are about twenty minutes from Haymarket. I would imagine this looks like home?" He points out the window.

"Yeah, so far." I keep staring at the window, hoping to see something different, but so far nothing much has changed.

"Keep yer eyes out. When we get to Haymarket, I would imagine you'll see something different. It'll be the older parts of town. I'll drive ye through Grassmarket. You Americans love it around there. That area was an inspiration for that very popular children's book about wizards.

You'll see the view to Edinburgh Castle from down there too."

He chatters on and on about how *Harry Potter* brought Scotland on the market and the rain starts to fall as we get closer into the city. I notice the buildings are starting to look more historic and cobblestone roads are littered below us as we drive through smaller roads.

"It's remarkable, isn't it?" Calum interrupts my thoughts as I take in the city. "I'll park down below if ye feel like a walk. That flight must've been claustrophobic."

I quietly nod because I've never seen something like this before. The buildings around home don't look anything like this. Different shapes and colors with windy roads. The streets look alive, with people moving along, without a care in the world. The city looks old—not in a dilapidated way, but in a way that feels like it holds wonderful stories behind it. I read about the rich history of Scotland and the fight for independence. Her people were about endurance and courage. I open my window to get a better peek of the city around me.

"Magical, right? I've lived in Edinburgh most of my life. This city is wonderful, even if I miss a wee bit of the Highlands."

"Are they far?" I stick my head out a little farther.

"No lad, not far at all. Now, this is Grassmarket coming up right now. I'll park and we can pop in the Black Bull for a bit of drink and food. Ye must be hungry too. And if ye fancy, we can walk up to the Royal Mile if yous like?" I turn to answer Calum and he's got a big smile on his face.

"It's not a problem?" I ask, because I don't want to waste his time.

"Like I said, Mr. Cardona has me at your service for the next few days. I would love to show you my country. And if ye like, and yer not tired. I can even drive ye up to the

Highlands, towards Inverness, and stop off at a few of the castles along the way. Inverness and Blackness are very nice castles."

"I—"

"I promise, lad, it's no problem. I would love to show ye around. I'll even bring the missus. She loves driving along, if ye don't mind?"

"Of course!"

"She's much better at telling history than I am." He smiles softly and starts to talk about his wife and two kids, who are all grown up. One of them still lives in Edinburgh and the other lives in London as a barrister, which I found out is a lawyer. Lunch at the Black Bull was wonderful. Calum had me order some haggis since it's traditional, and I'm always up for a challenge. I enjoyed everything, except the *mushy peas*, which I found very odd. Not sure why they go to the trouble of mashing them when peas taste fine without the extra work.

After lunch, we walk up a long, curvy road, with brightly colored stacked buildings. They're a unique mix of stores Calum says were the inspiration for *Harry Potter*. It was filled with eclectic stores, like a joke shop, candy shop, and even a witch's store. We continue up towards something Calum calls the Royal Mile. As soon as we take a turn up George IV Bridge, I see more and more crowding towards the street ahead of us.

"So, this is the Royal Mile. Very touristy but a lot of rich history. This thoroughfare links Edinburgh Castle all the way to Holyroodhouse Palace, which is a few miles down to the left, while from here, ye can obviously see Edinburgh Castle."

"The architecture is amazing." I must look like a deer caught in headlights because I've never seen anything like it. Walking through the streets, Edinburgh had a sort of crazy cool vibe. Old mixed with new, and everything in between. I can see why Calum said this area is very touristy, because almost every other shop caters to tourists. It's littered with a lot of similar shops, with trinkets and knickknacks.

"There are a lot of wool shops. Are they popular clothes to wear in the area?" I ask Calum as we walk through one of the shops. The store is quite small, white and gothic-looking, but as soon as we open the doors, there are lines upon lines of wool shawls and hats.

"Aye, well, Scotland has more sheep than people, ye see. We've got well over 14,000 farms scattered about the country." He picks up one of the wool shawls and inspects it. I watch as his lips purse, something about the shawl seems to have upset him. "We should leave, I'll take ye further up the road."

As we walk out of the store, Calum pulls something out of his jacket pocket. It's a small notebook. He makes note of something, then tucks it back into his jacket. "I wouldn't buy from them, the craftmanship wasnae good. When we take the drive up North, I have a friend who owns a shop. He carries beautiful shawls. Not to sound biased."

"I was thinking my Ma would like to have something like that. The winters get kinda cold from where I'm from."

"Aye, ye cannae find better wool than around these parts. I think yer mum would love it. We'll find ye a good one to take home, and at a better cost." He spits on the ground, disgusted by what he saw in that store. "And that price… A cheat, if ye ask me."

He continues muttering to himself about how ridiculous the price was. I want to laugh but I really don't want to insult him. As a tourist, I appreciate *not* being cheated, but I want to believe everywhere I go, no matter where in the world, there will be touristy shops that want to inflate prices.

"Calum, are we able to see the university from here?"

Calum stops and looks around and shakes his head. "No lad, the university is about a ten to fifteen-minute walk from here, but further down that way." He turns and points behind us.

"So, closer towards where we started from then." I look around, realizing these streets would be a good run path when I needed to let off some steam.

"Aye, lad, but further down. And the streets up these parts are fairly safe to run on. Just mind the cars."

"Huh?"

He laughs mirthlessly at me. "Ye said that out loud. Just make sure ye got yourself some good running shoes. These streets can be brutal, especially the cobble. But I think you'll be fine. Look fit."

I chuckle at his 'look fit' comment. "Yeah, I run a bit when back home."

"That's good. Now if ye go straight from here, New College is there and a wee bit up is the Scottish National Gallery. Ye can ring around and make yer way further up, and Princes Street Gardens takes a bit of space up. The Robert Louis Stevenson Memorial is at the far end. You can even see the back-end of Edinburgh Castle from there. It's all a good running area."

We continue our way up through the areas he mentioned, and I can see why he brought up the gardens. They span a good deal of ways down, and the view of the castle is amazing. Everything is green, and the flowers are all blooming. People are lounging around the benches that are placed throughout the gardens. Calum doesn't seem to slow down as we ring down King's Stables Road, where we get a closer look at the castle walls. I can see why this particular castle was considered a fortress in its time. The walls are incredibly high, and it sits above the rest of the city. I can't imagine any fight taking place here could've gone well.

As we make our way back towards the Royal Mile, I hear a lonely bagpipe echoing in the distance. Calum is smiling as we get closer to the pipes. A single man is wearing a kilt, and what Calum calls a belted plaid, which he says is very traditional.

"Since yer 'ere, if ye like the bagpipes, it would be good to get tickets to the Royal Edinburgh Military Tattoo during the Fringe, which starts in a few weeks. Aye, a bonnie good time."

"Ummmm… the Fringe?"

"Aye, the Fringe. It's a month-long arts festival that consumes the city. A lot of the street performers will be out too. My eldest bairn used to love for us to take her the Fringe every year." He points out different things around the city and I get a better grasp about the layout. It's a mixture of old and new.

As promised, I spend the next several days touring the country with Calum and his wife. I quickly fall in love with the land, and its people.

CHAPTER two

WEARING JUST A PAIR OF jeans and a blouse across campus is stupid. I'd spent all night studying ahead for my Statistics class I have at the end of the week. I know Charlotte will complain I was being a complete geek for studying for a class I've yet to take, but every studying hour was important. I had only enough time to brush my teeth, throw on whatever had been lying around, and tie my hair up in a messy bun. I looked unkempt, but I wasn't going to call up the ire of Professor Steward, who taught history. It was worth not having my jumper, *maybe*.

He's a renown historian, bloody brilliant, but tough as nails and *never* excuses a tardy. Even though I'm a business major, I wanted to take his class since he had wonderful take on historical economics around the world. As my nan always said, *ball's on the slates* if you're late to class, and she was right. Impressions are important, and I don't want things to be game over before I even get a chance to show my talents off, both in business and in the rest of my classes. Lessons I learned hard from my family. I was raised to work hard in everything I do. That meant one hundred percent, and no MacDonald was going to give less than that.

The professor's lecture was bloody brilliant, and despite my kerfuffle with my clothes, I'd aced my summer paper for the class, the topic of which was the historical study of America's Great Depression and the economic downturn seen throughout Western Europe. I even got a nod in adding a little of my lessons learned in Macroeconomics from last quarter. With class being over, I decide to stroll about outside. Pushing hard against the heavy doors, I almost backed up from the chill that ran through my body as the cold, wet wind hit me in the face. *Damn it.* The dreaded weather is going on again.

As delusional as it may seem, I thought I was safe to walk the grounds without something warmer. I've lived in Scotland my whole life, and any Scot knows, we can have four seasons in one day. It can be a bit dewy in the morning, boiling hot by mid-morning, and then by afternoon tea, it can be snowing. The weather here is ridiculous, but I love it. Being in city as old as dirt, with such a rich history, has a surprise around every corner. Even my English friends, who now attend university here, remark on the city as being quaint. It's busy, but still has a feel of being an enclosed small town. I can walk in peace, with the sprinkling of gardens throughout the city, or pop up to the Royal Mile for stroll through the past, with the touristy man blowing away at his bagpipes and fake William Wallace made famous by Hollywood.

I'm truly chuffed about this year. The dean of the business college has taken on the biggest undertaking we've seen in all the years I've attended university. My Da wanted me to go to Cambridge or Oxford, but I wanted to stay here in

Scotland. We had a row over it during my fourth year. I had the pick of the lot, but Edinburgh at the time made sense— I absolutely loved the city and many of my friends chose to attend. My Da didn't think it was illustrious enough, but I had won out.

Case in point, if I'd attended any of the other universities he suggested, I wouldn't be able to partake in this year's program. We have six prestigious visiting Business and Economics professors from around the world, who would be teaching a handful of handpicked students from the business college, including me. My advisor told me last semester I was the first picked amongst the department to partake in the program this year.

I decide to quickly pop into the coffee shop around the corner from the business building. I must caffeinate myself or I'll end up wanting to take a nap, which is the worst thing I can do today. The sky is beginning to clear, but just barely, which means it'll probably continue to be a bit nippy to run around campus with no jumper.

I breeze right through the door and thank God there are no lines. As soon as I see who's working the counter, I can't help but smile.

"Hey, Jonathan!" I wave enthusiastically to my favorite barista, which only makes him snort laugh.

"Hey beautiful, popping in for yer usual?" He begins to make my drink of choice, which he's memorized since I'm easily here at least three or four times a day.

"Well, I don't know? Maybe I want something different." I look at the chalkboard written down with today's special, which is some ridiculous toffee type coffee. I wince, because toffee in coffee is a tragedy. I smirk at Jonathan's frown. He plops the pot of milk he was about to steam onto the counter.

"Now, now. Do girls have tits?"

"*What*?! Why would ye ask me that, of course girls have tits, ye idiot." I laugh as his mouth thins and I can tell by the way he's holding himself up, he's trying to control his laugh.

"I just wanted to get ye to say tits. Proper Scottish lass like yerself, such a dirty mouth." His brows cock up and down as he laughs and sticks the milk under the coffee steamer.

"Yer so crass." I roll my eyes. "But seriously, maybe I wanted something different…like tea." I finger the tea bags along the counter. The store is fairly small—maybe less than three people can work behind the counter easily—and the walls are bright yellow. There are a handful of chairs and tables where students can meet up. Every once in a while, when I need to be kept fully caffeinated, I'll do my studying here but generally, I just do a grab and go.

"Here ye go, beautiful. Ye break my heart every time ye come in here with that beautiful fiery hair." He has my mocha latte in hand and his eyes are burning brightly at me. Jonathan is giving me *that* look. It's the look he has when I know he's about to ask me out on a date. While he's a good-looking guy, I really don't have time to date at the moment. Plus, I can't afford to piss off my favorite coffee guy. I'd have to go further up for coffee if things go badly, and they *always* go badly. My Da said my personality is as wild as my hair. Most of the guys I've dated over the years think I'm too independent. Ultimately, they try to *change* me or mold me into someone I'm not.

"Jonathan…" I groan.

"Don't worry about it, Isla, a man's gotta dream… dirty dreams, of course." He winks and hands me my coffee. I laugh and take a sip of the warm liquid. As soon as the sweetness of the dark chocolate hits my tongue, I groan again.

"Jesus, Isla, get out." I pop my eyes open and grin at Jonathan, who's shaking his head. I'm sure that groan won him a little spank bank time tonight. I quickly wave goodbye and pop back onto the street. The weather has gotten cooler, and I tuck in a little closer to my warm coffee.

I have a large gap between classes, so I could go back to the library to do some more studying, but I already feel a little stuffy at the moment. I decide to turn back and walk on over to the Meadows, where I know Finn and the guys will be having their rugby practice. Even with the dreary day, Finn, who is captain of the rugby football club, would be forcing his guys to practice.

I see the guys as I get closer and, squinting, I see a fairly tall guy I don't recognize. He's got no shirt on, and his hair looks tossed about and curly. Finn is wearing the most ridiculous bright shirt I've ever seen him in. He and I attended the same schools, though, he was a year ahead of me. The guy is a bit cheeky and likes to flash about it. Finn's eyes meet mine as I move off the path and onto the grass, and he flashes me a big smile and nods as he runs down the field. The guy he'd been talking to runs with him. I watch as Finn flings his arms about as the ball gets tossed behind him to the stranger, who catches the ball. I wince when I see Hal charging towards him. The man has his head down and doesn't see Hal. Even though he seems to be running fairly fast, and quickly dodging the rest of the guys, no one can get past Hal when he's like this. Finn screams at the guy to pick his head up, but it's too late. Hal charges forward and grabs him at his waist, and tosses him like a rag doll.

"Who's that chap that just got hit?" I turn and see my roommate, Charlotte, next to me. I hadn't even noticed she'd come up to see the boys. I take a sip of my coffee and sigh.

"Dunno, never seen him before. Maybe Finn's got a

new team member to train. He's shite though, if ye ask me."

The guys are moving into position down the field again, now that Hal knocked the ball clear from that guy's hands.

"He doesn't look pleased with himself… or Hal." Charlotte giggles, and I turn to see her cheeks glow pinker.

"Ugh, ye like him, don't ye."

"Oh my God, Isla, how can ye *not* like him?"

"He could be a tosser. And he isn't much of a pitchman, if ye ask me."

"Who the fuck cares! Look at his chest and that cut. He can toss and twirl me any day of the week. Plus, I bet ye he has big hands." She giggles some more.

All I can do is try to ignore Charlotte. She is completely boy crazy. I've been her roommate at Uni for the last two years. She's always on the arm of a new guy every few months. I asked her once why, and she just shrugged and said these were the years she was supposed to sample the goods before settling down. She called it *buffet dating*. You taste something, and if you don't like it, you can throw it away. But if it tasted good, you can keep going back for more. She's crass, but I love her.

"God, look at him. He's so yummy, Isla." She fans her burning face and I laugh at her worse than normal behavior. "I want to lick him like a grand Crunchie. Glistening glorious of man, and that smile."

I can't help but spit out my coffee. "Jesus, Charlotte, are ye in heat?" I wipe the little bit of coffee off my mouth.

"Yes, so why can't a girl be in lust? Boys do it all the time, Isla." She hip thrusts a little to emphasize her point, and one of the players runs by, tripping over his feet when he notices Charlotte showing off.

I wipe my eyes as the guy continues tripping over

himself, while Charlotte winks at him and gives her breasts a squeeze. "I really can't take ye anywhere."

"Say ye love me, Isla. Why else ye put up with me and even braid my hair in the mornings, like the best friend I know ye to be."

"I love ye, but yer too much sometimes." We continue watching the boys running through their practice. The *hottie*, as Charlotte keeps referring to him as, keeps mucking up a bit. He is terrible and I'm not sure why Finn is putting up with him. Edinburgh is geared to be on top this year, so Finn is just wasting time with this lad.

Finn has the ball and again, he tosses it to the stranger. With quick feet, *the hottie* manages to dodge Hal. Before he can get hit by another player, the guy lifts his arm but instead of tossing the ball back or to the side, he swings his arm up and throws the ball forward.

"For fuck's sake, ye bawbag! What do ye think yer doing!?" I shout out, my arms flailing. I screamed out so loud, all the guys stop and stare at where the noise came from. Finn is laughing as I run onto the field, because no Scotsman would dare throw that ball forward. I don't know what he was thinking, but if Finn isn't going to kick this bloke off the team, I'm going to *make* him.

The stranger with tossed hair and a glistening chest is staring back at me as I rush over. His hazel-green eyes are confused about what is happening, which makes me even more mad. I don't even give Finn any time to talk before I rat on.

"Ye eejit, ye *never* toss forward! What were ye thinking?"

CHAPTER *three*

BEN

I DID IT AGAIN. I'VE never played rugby. *Ever.* When I applied to attend the university, I'd only been given my roommate's name and an email address. I'd contacted Finn Campbell the first week I'd received his information, and we exchanged communication a few times before I'd arrived, so I knew a little about him. He wasn't due to be on campus until a few days before classes began, so when I arrived into the city, I had the room all to myself.

Calum and his wife were a true blessing in disguise. I'd gotten an opportunity to leave the city and travel around the country. Before I knew it, Scotland had stolen my heart. There was something truly magical about the Highlands, with its high green hills that went on for miles, and the scattered lochs.

When Calum said there were more sheep than people, he wasn't kidding. hills throughout the country were littered with them. I still don't know how any farmer could keep track of them, but Calum assured me it was a centuries old system that still worked today.

I'd been to see Blackness Castle, then all the way over to Stirling Castle, where I learned the *real* history of Scotland through Mrs. Macrae, who I later learned was a retired History professor. She had a wonderful way of retelling history as if I were living it, and not some retold history through movies.

I'd seen Culloden on my third day in the country. Unfortunately, Mrs. Macrae couldn't come along since she promised a friend she'd have lunch, but Calum was not short of tales. For a battlefield, Culloden seemed very flat. There was a feeling of sadness that washed over me. It was as if all the souls who had perished there were singing out their tales to me. Calum said it wasn't an abnormal feeling when I asked him about it. It was a *connection* he said, that some visitors get. He seemed pleased I'd been enjoying my time here. I was sad my days with them were coming to an end, but Calum and Mrs. Macrae assured me I was to not be a stranger.

Before Finn arrived, I'd received a very large care package from them, full of snacks and drinks, with a very nice note about me doing good this year. When Finn finally arrived, he'd seen the open care package full of snacks. He'd been keen on me sharing, which I was glad to, since I didn't know what half of the snacks were. I almost choked on Irn Bru, which was like an overly sweetened carbonated orangesicle. I handed the rest over to Finn, who was more than happy to drink all of it.

I immediately liked him, even if I couldn't understand him half the time. On that first afternoon, I'd caught him watching some sort of game that looked like a hybrid of football and soccer. When I asked him what he was watching, he'd been shocked I'd never seen rugby. Case in point, why I'm on this field at the moment. I'd learned he was captain of the rugby club here at the university. I was a solo type of workout guy, who preferred running or boxing, so team sports weren't really my thing. After he learned that I loved to run, he insisted that I come out to the field to learn.

Finn laughs at me after I threw the ball forward for the second time. I still can't quite get the whole throwing to the side or backwards. It all seems moronic.

"Finn, who the hell is that girl? Did she just say *ball-bag*?" It all kind of got muddled, after taking a hit from one of the other team members.

"Shite, don't mind that bonnie lass. That's just Isla MacDonald. Her family is a patron of the university, and her Da's a huge rugby lover. And not *ball bag*, she said bawbag. It's what ye Americans call scrotum. It's not very polite either. It's meant to be an insult, but Isla is just—"

Michael, who is on my left, is laughing his ass off as the fiery redhead comes out onto the field. *Patron*. That puts my hackles up. I've met people like her. Harvard had plenty of upper-class egomaniacs. Students who thought the world revolved around them, making them believe they could run their mouths to whatever and whomever. I knew how to deal with them.

Finn doesn't get a chance to finish since the girl is shouting even louder. Even the people walking on the side have stopped to watch.

"Seriously, what the fuck is her problem?" I spit out before she reaches me. As she rushes forward, I get a better look at her. She's absolutely gorgeous, almost like a dream. She's what Toby would call a knockout, even though he much prefers brunettes but hides his preferences with blondes. As she gets closer, I get a better look at her face, which is covered with freckles, and she has bright blue eyes and pink-reddish lips. I could tell they were natural-colored, but it's as if God painted them the perfect shade to be kissed.

"Finn, what the bloody hell are ye doing?" Her anger is directed at Finn, who is smirking at this fireball of a woman.

"Ahhh, Isla, come on, lass. It's just a bit of a game." He swings his arms around her and gives her a little nudge. I'd almost think they were dating, except she wasn't eyeing Finn with lovesick puppy eyes, but something else.

"Bit of game?" She's beginning to fluster. "You cannae be serious? He cannae even play. What Scotsman would toss the ball forward?" She shoves Finn off of her, and I'm convinced she's seriously off her rocker.

"Now, lass, yer bum's oot the windae! You should calm down; dinnae ye worry yer little head off." Finn is just smirking at her, amused at her tantrum. Truly, I hope not all Scottish women are this uptight.

"Finn—"

"Come on, Sweet Cheeks. Finn is just teaching me a bit of the game." I saccharinely smile at her, hoping she'll stop yelling, because everyone is staring now.

"Oh…" I watch as she slow blinks up at me. Her cheeks begin to glow more rosy, mixing in with her already prominent freckled face. Her messy bun is askew, bits of her bright red hair flowing in her face. She slowly tucks the whispies behind her hair and eyes Finn, who is chuckling to himself. "He's not from here?" she whispers softly to Finn, who just nods his head.

"Nahhh, babe. Not from here, so if you don't mind toning it down a bit. Your screaming surely could be heard all the way down the road." I smile and Michael tosses me the ball.

"Babe?" Her voice rises slightly, and I hear a tone of

annoyance. I could leave her alone, but I enjoy watching her get more and more flustered.

"Yeah, you know. Babe, Sweet Cheeks, or maybe I'll call you Wildfire. Like a spitting mad fire." I laugh and toss the ball back to Michael. The guys shuffle off to the side to grab some water. If I didn't know better, I'd think they don't want to be around when she blows up again.

"I'm Ben, by the way, but I'm not impartial to you naming me Hot Stuff. By the way, these abs are nice and hard. You can touch them if you want. Seeing that you're staring at them." I smile down at her.

"Wankpig! I wasnae staring at ye!"

"Oh, sweetheart, I believe you were." I rub my abs, just to make a point, and her gaze slips to where my hands are. I cock my brow, waiting to see if she notices what she's doing.

"Ughhhh! Arse." She stomps her foot and I can't help but laugh.

"You're such a foul-mouth for a little thing. Maybe I can teach you proper etiquette… with my mouth." I smirk at her before walking away. She's way too easy of a target, and personally, I was having too much fun riling her up.

"She's up to high doh." Finn falls in line with me when I grab my water I left on the sidelines.

"I don't know what that means, because back at home, we have another saying." I take a long drink of the nice, cool water. Finn just shakes his head.

"Aye, she's just working herself up. She wants us to win just as much as I do. Ignore Isla. She's just being Isla. Once you get to know her, gettin' past the rough exterior, she's really a bonnie lass."

He slaps my back and I take another swig of my drink. I don't know if I believe him so much, but Finn seems to be a pretty good guy. I turn and see a sour look on Isla's face, as a tall woman with long, wavy brown hair, and doe eyes walks towards us. She's got a big smile on her face and she shakes her head at Isla, who makes a face right back at her. A few of the guys nod their head towards her, and Finn, who had been walking over to them, turns and makes a beeline for her.

I decide to take a chance and introduce myself, hoping I don't get my head chewed off. The new girl who showed up, turns to me and smiles.

"Hi, handsome, I'm Charlotte." I reach out to shake her hand while Isla folds her arms.

"Charlotte, nice to meet you…" I glance over. Isla has her jaw clenched and her fists are closed tight, as if she wants to hit someone.

"Isla, calm down. I'm just saying hi. He's not the enemy, even if he's an American." She smiles even wider and seems to be poking fun of Isla, who appears to be biting her tongue.

"So, since you lasses are here. How about some bevvies later? We have to finish practice. Give us a little time to get ready, don't want you nice lasses to smell us from a mile away. I'm pretty rank meself." Finn speaks up, and Charlotte squeals, clapping her hands.

"Yes! Isla and I will both be there." She turns towards Isla and gives her nudge and a wink.

"I can't—"

"Don't be a snob, Isla, just come out. It's the beginning of term and I know yer ahead of studies already. I want to hang with my best girl, my best guy, and this cutie. I have questions about America. Never been." Her eyes are alight and she's giving Isla a look. Isla shakes her head, so Charlotte grabs her hand and tugs her away from us.

I watch as Isla throws her arms up and starts pointing to us, and Charlotte begins to pout. They both are speaking so softly to each other, but I can't make out what they're saying.

"Dude, what is up with the redhead?" I hiss. "I don't want to go out with them if she's like that."

Finn narrows his eyes at them and folds his arms over his chest. "Like I said earlier, she's good lass. I *promise*. She's just a bit guarded, is all. She doesn't take well to strangers. I'll talk to ye about her later when we get ready. I don't want to her to overhear me."

He keeps glancing over at them. For a second, I think he's annoyed with me but I notice a look pass between him and Charlotte. Isla has her head turned and she's looking further down the field. Charlotte winks at Finn, who lets out the breath he'd been holding.

Charlotte walks back with Isla in tow. "Finn, darling, we will be there—" Charlotte side-glares at Isla. "Both of us."

Finn nods his head and gives Isla a look. Something cracks between the two, but Charlotte seems so distracted and doesn't notice Finn staring at her.

"Well, I'll be going off with Isla now, and be talking about ye boys when we go." Charlotte giggles and Isla looks up at her with a scowl on her face.

"Charlotte," she hisses. "Stop. I told ye I would go, why do ye have to blab that out to everyone."

Her gaze flicks upward towards me and I just smirk at her. I swear, more freckles have popped up on her face, and I cannot tell if she's embarrassed or about to get mad at me again. She narrows her eyes at me a little longer than what would be appropriate or comfortable, then smiles nicely to Finn and turns her back to me in a huff. Before Charlotte can catch up, Finn grabs Charlotte around the waist, which makes her stop in her tracks. He leans in and whispers something in her ear. A rosy-colored blush begins to bloom around her neck, up to her cheeks. Her lip trembles a little and she nods her head, then turns and runs after Isla, who seems to be speed walking off the field.

"What was all that about?"

Finn keeps staring off at them. "Staking my claim." He turns and around and smiles at me. "I'll see ye back at the dorms, Dunn. Hope ye had a good time, but Isla is right, the guys and I need to be in ship-shape form to be on top."

He waves goodbye and I smirk. I was right about him and Charlotte. I quickly grab for my shirt and water bottle and decide to go for a run.

FINN WALKS IN WITH A TOWEL WRAPPED AROUND HIS WAIST. He'd been gone a few hours and when he'd walked into the room to grab his bath things, I swear someone dragged in the dumpster. He quickly apologized and said he ran into some mud during practice.

"So, about Isla…"

I put down the book I'd been studying and look at Finn, who is drying his hair with his towel. I just mumble something incoherent because clearly, this conversation was on the back of his mind.

"I've known her since grade school. Her family and I have been friends for many years." He continues getting ready, messing about in his closet. "She's the eldest daughter of Craig MacDonald, he's one of our finest businessmen in the country."

"Wait, you're talking about *the* Craig MacDonald. Holy shit."

Finn laughs at me as he puts on his boxers.

"So, ye Americans do keep up with us a bit?" He smiles and folds his arms over his chest.

"I'm an Economics major at Harvard. We studied about

the huge business deal struck between his firm and the largest conglomerated company in London. In my world, he's a big deal."

"Aye, and what do ye think that does to a girl like Isla? I don't want to talk out of turn, since we just met, but I saw ye eyeing her when she came up the field. She is a bonnie lass, always has been, but her personality can be…" His mouth thins.

"Difficult?" I cock my brow.

"Aye, difficult, yes, but more than that. Craig MacDonald didnae raise Isla to be anything but independent. He comes from a proud family. Isla could've gone anywhere around the world. She chose Scotland. I can imagine the row she had with her Da about that."

"What do you mean? Edinburgh is not a second-class university. Yins are ranked." I grab hold of my cup of water I left on the nightstand and take a sip.

"What's a yins?" Finn pops his head out of his closet and is looking at me, confused.

"Yins? It means you all." I smile and shrug.

"Aye, ye Americans all sound so different." He just laughs and tucks back into his closet, looking for some clothes.

"So, what are you saying, that Isla is just being proud?"

"Aye, not just that. I watched that bonnie lass with some of the other boys…" He pauses, like he's trying to be careful of what he's about to say.

The hairs on the back of my neck stand up, because I swear, if someone hurt her, I may need to punch something.

"Did someone hurt her?" My tone raises an octave as I voice my concern, and Finn turns back with his shirt in his hand.

He shakes his head. "Ah dinnae ken."

"Huh? I don't know what that means." There are times

Finn's accent gets thicker and harder to understand. "Does that mean no, or you don't know?"

"Ah, sorry. It means, I don't know. At least, I hope not. Isla seems like a girl that can handle herself. She'd have me balls ripped off, I would imagine, if I touched her unwanted." He shrugs. "But they didn't treat her right either. Isla is so headstrong. The guys she went out with wanted her to act a certain way. Thought they could get her to change. Didnae seem right. She's not the kind of lass that would change, even for a man. *Especially* for a man. So, don't mind her. She may come from good stock, but she's also a good person inside. Just takes a bit of time to get to know her."

He starts to whistle as he gets ready. It doesn't look like he is dressing up, which is good since I don't feel like putting anything fancy on. It's a jeans and nice shirt kind of night for me.

CHAPTER *four*

Isla

"I SLA, DOES THIS MAKE ME look fat?"

I look up from the book I'd been reading and see Charlotte wearing a sleeveless dark navy dress that dips fairly low. She can get away with a more daring dress in the front because she doesn't have *"Barbie boobs,"* as she likes to say. Where the dress is tight at the top, it flows out at the waist, with cute pockets. If I was so inclined to dress up, it's the kind of dress I would want to wear. Fancy, yet comfortable. With pockets, no less.

"Isla, earth to Isla. What do you think?" She twirls a little and the bottom of the dress billows a little up. It's not immodest at all. It's *perfect.*

"Ye look absolutely beautiful, Charlotte… And no, ye don't look fat. Yer being ridiculous." I smile and look back down at the book I'd been reading.

"Truly? I don't look like a right cow." She's flattening

the dress out in front our full-length mirror, shifting from foot to foot and turning.

"Oh my God, Charlotte, why are ye so nervous all of a sudden?" I close my book and set it aside, then glance over at the clock. I'm running out of time and probably should get ready. As soon as I agreed to join everyone to the pub, I refused to acknowledge Ben. I was already embarrassed I'd lost my temper once already, and something about him put my hair up.

"I don't know, it's the first of term and I want to make sure… I don't know, God, I sound pretentious." She dusts off her perfectly clean dress and starts to look around for what shoes to wear.

I laugh at her getting flustered. She's not one to get like this. I've seen her flirt with the best of them, and *never* cares how she looks most of the time. She's the kind of girl who likes to dress herself up for herself and no one else, but something seems terribly off. "Charlotte, seriously, what's up?"

I sit still and watch her, throwing shoes about, and grimace at the mess she's making. I love her dearly, but she is not one to pick up after herself. I don't even think she notices everything is usually placed back to where it supposed to be after she leaves our rooms.

"I just… Ah dinnae ken. Finn just said something that sort of threw me off, is all." She begins to twirl her hair around her finger, which is a total tell. She only does that when something is making her nervous.

I smile. Finally. I've been waiting for three years for Finn to do something. Every time I run into him, he always asks how Charlotte's doing. I knew after the first few asks, he must've liked her, but never seemed to ask her out. It's like he was waiting for something but he would never tell me what.

"Did he ask ye on a date?" I ask, hoping she'd just spill the beans already. I really think they would do well together. He's more pragmatic while she's a little more outgoing.

"Ah dinnae ken." She stands up after finding a pair of dark red Chanels and slips them on.

"What do ye mean, 'ah dinnae ken'? It's not rocket science, Charlotte." She moves towards the mirror and bites down on her lower lip. "Ye should wear those other dark-red flats I saw ye in before term ended. The pub is in the older part of town, and a bit of a walk, even if we take a cab."

"Are ye sure? This dress feels like it needs something else." She taps her foot.

"Yeah, I'm sure. Put those cute bangle bracelets on. The stackable ones, and I think you'll be good to go."

I get up to grab a pair of my dark denim jeans. I refuse to wear a dress to the pub, there doesn't seem to be a reason to, so I go with something simple. I pull out my boots from the closet and when I turn around, Charlotte is standing right behind me.

"Jesus, Charlotte, what the fuck. Ye scared the shite out of me." I place my hand over my heart, waiting for it to slow down.

"I like him." She moves back a few steps, hands shifting her bracelets excessively.

"There isn't anything wrong with him liking ye, Charlotte. Yer a nice girl and he's a nice boy. I don't see a problem with this."

She begins to shake her head, like everything I'm telling her is wrong. She mutters something to herself, so low I can't make it out. I grab her hands to make her stop flipping her bracelets back and forth.

"What did ye say?"

Her fingers tremble at my touch. "I just… I've liked him

for a long time. He's never shown interest before, so I didn't think—" She shakes her head and her bottom lip begins to wobble.

"Ye didnae think he liked ye? Seriously, Charlotte, he's liked ye for years." Her eyes look up to mine and I see a lone teardrop has fallen onto her cheek. I smile at my best friend. "I think he's been waiting for a good time to just ask ye out. Yer kind of the unattainable gal, the boys are always surrounding ye." She begins to open her mouth to refute what I'm about to say, so I cut her off. "I know that's not something ye can help. Yer smart, yer beautiful, inside and out, so you naturally attract guys, like bees to honey." I hand her a tissue and she dabs at her cheek.

"Bit of advice from yer bestie. Just be yerself. Yer lucky to have a guy who likes ye for *you*, and not some imaginary pedestal of ye. He's had years to watch and get to know ye from afar, so get to know him. He's a good guy, Charlotte. I'm happy for ye."

I turn my back to her. I love that two people I've known for years might've found each other, but I won't lie, it also stings a little. I've known Finn much longer than Charlotte. He comes from a good family, and even for a guy with money, he doesn't flaunt nor is he pretentious, like some of the other people I grew up with. He would treasure the person she is and for me, that is everything. A guy who loves you despite yourself. I've never found anyone like that. Over the years, I thought maybe if I was little more amenable, I would find the love I deserve. I tried it a few times, being someone I'm not, just to make everyone around me happy. But trying to be different for the sake of being different made me miserable. As my mum said, "Yer just not made for it." And she was right, I was old enough to know who I am.

"Oh, Isla, you'll find someone too." Charlotte hugs me

from behind and I look at her in the mirror. Her normal bright eyes seem sad. Sad for me. She knows what a struggle it's been dating guys around University.

"I'm too stubborn for my own good." I smile and pat her hand. "Now that ye had yer cry out, come help me put myself together. Ye know I can't do makeup." Charlotte nods and gives me one last squeeze before she starts to flit about, pulling out her makeup palette.

"God, Isla, ye were right. I'm so glad I wore the flats. These stones are ridiculous, I *hate* Edinburgh. I would've tanked if I wore my Chanels." We are both strolling our way up the street. The taxis can't come up this way as the streets are too narrow, so they drop us off at the bottom of the hill. Charlotte keeps cursing about how her legs are straining.

"Bite yer tongue, ye should never say ye hate this city, Charlotte. It's not that bad." I smile as I lean a little more forward to ease my way up.

"Not bad… Not bad, my calves are burning. I'd only want them to burn like this is if I was squatting on top of a guy, Isla." She snorts laughs and I grab her arm before she trips forward. She's so uncoordinated. Bless Finn. Another reason these two will do well together. He'll always be there to catch her clumsy arse.

"Phew, thanks, bestie. Do ye think anyone saw that?" She turns and sees a few people milling about below us.

Gasping, I stop and slap my chest. "Oh dear."

"What?" Charlotte has a horrified look on her face. She's tugging down her dress as if pulling will make it longer. "Do ye think anyone can see my fancy panties? I wore them special for Finn."

I nearly take a tumble as my foot hits a slight crack on the sidewalk. "Jesus, Mary. Charlotte, can ye be any more blasé about these things."

"I like to say I'm being honest. If Finn fancies me, I want to make sure I look good underneath this dress."

I roll my eyes at her absurdity. I don't know if Finn would immediately take her home. He seems like the kind of guy who would want to take her on a date first before jumping in.

"Don't roll yer eyes. Ye can be such a nun sometimes, Isla. We are young and free to do what we want. And like ye said, Finn is a nice guy. I don't want to waste any more time dicking about." She flattens her dress as we finally make it to the top where the pub sits. The rugby club likes to come up this way, since it's not as touristy, being off the beaten path. The owners are a local couple who've owned this establishment for as long as I can remember coming here. My Da used to bring me up after some of the games.

"Ye look fine, Charlotte. Makeup and hair look perfect. He knows what ye look like and I'm a hundred percent positive he likes what he sees. Come on, before the pints get warm."

I push open the old wooden doors. I have to put my weight into it, as they are heavy wooden doors surrounded by metal slats that give it an *antique* look. The color is almost black but on closer inspection, it's a very dark brown shade. As we walk in, I can hear familiar tunes lightly playing in the background. I love this pub, from the looks to the clientele. It's local, through and through. Heavy lighting drops down from the ceiling, giving the pub a warm golden glow. There are tables mixed in with bench-like tables, allowing for larger groups to hang out. The bar itself sits in the middle of the pub where patrons can order their bevvies and food.

Charlotte nudges me out of my trance; I'd been staring the coming and goings where the bar sat. "What?"

"The guys are over there, waving us down." She waves at them and grabs my arm, pulling me towards the table. Not everyone on the rugby team have shown up. It's about a quarter of the team, which isn't surprising, since term is just starting to begin.

"Hey, Finn. Guys." Charlotte smiles widely at Finn and elbows me again. "Isla," she hisses, and I look up at her with my stink eye.

"Charlotte, stop elbowing me. Yer so bony it hurts."

"Ye were staring at that handsome American. What's his name again?" Charlotte links her arm around me.

"Ben. He said his name was Ben." I look around, hoping for a seat as far away from him as possible. There is one open seat next to Finn and Ben is sitting across him, with one seat open next to him. I groan because Charlotte would kill me if I sit next to Finn.

"Hey, ye want to sit across from Finn?" I ask for good measure, because maybe she would want to face him while talking.

Her face scrunches up and she shakes her head. "Are ye seriously kidding me? Isla, that had to be the stupidest thing ye have ever asked. Did ye trip and fall?"

"Charlotte—"

"Don't 'Charlotte' me, Isla. Haud yer wheesht, okay. Just shut up," she hisses.

I look over to the guys, who look a little perplexed as to why we are still standing. Finn waves us over and he's giving Charlotte excited puppy eyes while Ben is smirking at both of us. I seriously want to slap that smile off his face.

Charlotte quickly shuffles us closer to the table and shoves me around where Michael sits, forcing me to sit next to Ben, who starts to laugh as she rings back to her seat with Finn.

"Well, hello, Wildfire. Decided to make it, finally. Didn't think you'd show up, seeing that we've been here long enough to finish our pints and get halfway through the next."

He takes a swig of his dark ale and wipes away the beer dribbling down his mouth. God, he's such a pig.

"I see ye need a bib, American. Don't they teach you boys how to drink properly?" He has the gall to laugh out loud.

"Maybe, seeing us lowly Americans are so dirty, right? He takes another gulp of his beer.

"Hey, Isla, Finn is getting me a cider. Would ye like one too?" Charlotte is looking at me expectantly and mouths, "*Behave*," to me while Finn is whispering something in her ear. They are awfully close, but whatever he's telling her makes her blush.

"Ummm… Actually, do ye mind getting me two fingers of the Macallan, or Glenfiddich if they don't have that one?" I go to pull out some money from my pocket, but Finn waves me off. I can see Ben wince a little, as if my drink of choice offended him.

"What's wrong with whisky?" I clench my teeth as he tilts his head to stare at me. As if I were some animal he was observing.

He taps his chin, smiles, and then shakes his head. "I never expected a gal like you to drink scotch whisky."

"A girl like me?" I fold over my arms, annoyed at what he's implying at. "Ye mean, a girl with sophistication and not a beer-guzzling American who can't hold his liquor." I smile serenely at him.

"Don't patronize me. It's really unbecoming of you,

Isla." He spits out my name slowly, as if it were a curse. "Plus, what's up with snobby Scottish women?"

"I'm not snobbish."

Ben just laughs into his beer. "Could've fooled me. You've been like this from the first minute I met you. What about my *Americanism* bothers you so much? Hmmm? I think it's my good looks."

"I… am… not… snobbish." I slowly annunciate, so his stupid head pays attention. "Just because I like whisky and not beer? If ye took a second to ask, I dinnae like the bitter taste in my mouth." I try to calm down and be a little more polite despite us rowing back and forth. He's not helping things, especially after the dismal first impression.

"Hmmmm… well, with a mouth like yours, I'm surprised you don't like bitter." He laughs and slams down his glass harder than I think he meant to.

"What is that supposed to mean?" I turn to look at him because talking while not looking is quite rude. He cocks his brows up and down. It takes me a second to understand what he was suggesting. "Yer disgusting. What kind of bloke brings that up at a pub?"

"One that is interested, I guess." He grabs the chip off the plate in front of him and shoves it in his mouth. I must not have been paying attention, but looks like the guys had ordered some food.

"Ye couldnae pay me enough, with a gob like yers. I bet ye have a knob the size of my pinky. I like guys with a little more girth," I spit out in contempt. If I were honest, I wouldn't know if I like girth or not, seeing I've only been with two guys, and both were a disaster.

Ben's now glowering at me. His eyes look greener now I've had a closer look. Outside on the field, they looked brown and green, but inside the pub, with this lighting, they have a more golden-green hue. If he weren't so foul, I'd say he was very pretty, with his curly, light brown-golden hair, and scruff upon his face. He's the kind of guy I would be attracted to.

Ben leans in a little closer, his eyes glistening. "Oh, you wish you could feel this around your mouth."

He grabs his front area and gives it a squeeze, then flashes me his pearly white teeth. I can't help but roll my eyes at his audacity. Before I can pull back and slap him in the face, I see two older women standing behind him. They tap his shoulder and his attention moves to them.

CHAPTER *five*

GOD, SHE'S INFURIATING BUT SOMETHING about her willingness to spar back with me makes me hard, which is a terrible inconvenience at the moment. I wouldn't normally be so forward with someone I just met, and I certainly wouldn't have grabbed myself in public, but before I could stop myself, the words slipped from my lips. But something about making this wildfire blush harder made me do it.

Isla is anything but boring. My dating life is what it is, unlike Toby. I may flirt, but I don't dip into relationships without knowing I really like the girl. I'm no virgin, but I'm not a slut to my body, even if the girls hang off me like ornaments. I enjoy being around people and I wasn't going to be rude. I have two sisters, so most of my female friends know I would *always* be respectful. I'm the "go-to date" when they don't want to go alone.

I certainly don't want to make the same mistakes as my

father, who was charming to a fault. So charming, he'd left us behind for what he considered *better* things. More like younger girls.

I'm looking for the full package, a partner who has similar dreams to mine or, at the very least, understands where I'm planning to go. Most importantly, I want a girl who I can converse with. Meeting Isla was like getting smacked by a train running at full speed. I call her Wildfire for a reason. She burns hot and with purpose, but wildfire is terribly unpredictable and, at times, uncontrollable. While I don't fancy myself a controlling guy, I want to be able to at least hold on while also allowing her to flourish.

She's also beautiful to boot. Her haunting blue eyes are something out of this world. Deep, dark blue around the edges, but a hint of green ocean in the middle. She's like a siren calling out to me—dangerous and so alluring. I find myself wondering if I would ever get the opportunity to kiss every freckle she had. With so many painting her face, I wonder if they're all over her body.

But she hated me on the spot. I don't know how to *not* be myself around her. I could charm her, but I feel like that's a falsity. I want to win her by just being me. From what Finn told me, her family has long-standing financial and political ties to Scotland.

With all that pomp and circumstance, I could see through her after my talk with Finn. She didn't seem like the girls I knew back at home. While rich was a part of her, she didn't hold herself above anyone, even if she portrayed herself to be. Finn confirmed my assessment—while Isla went to all the great schools here, she also was very independent as they come. Finn said she could've gone to any school, but chose to stay at home because she loves this land. Spending just a little time here, I can see why.

While finishing up my run, I'd called Toby on the way

back to the dormitories. He begrudgingly picked up, as it was still fairly early in New York. When I mentioned I met a girl, he stopped groaning and told me to *speak*. After I told him I thought she hated me, he laughed his ass off for nearly ten minutes before calming down. *Asshole.* Even though Toby is the very last person I should talk to for advice, he just said to use my charming personality to win her over. Case in point, my *charming* turned into one part, creeper and two parts, asshole.

She hates me. I can see it in her face, in her tone of voice she used with me. I'm failing miserably.

The girls who just stopped by, asking me for a drink, are grad students. When I told them how old I was, they got even more excited.

"So, yer name is Ben?" The tall brunette leans over and I can smell the alcohol all over her breath.

"Ummm… yeah, Ben." I quickly grab her hands, which are dangerously close to the fly of my jeans. I was already hard after the little spat I had with Isla and I didn't want to give these ladies any ideas.

"Yer not from here, are ye?" She smiles down at me. I think she misunderstood why I'd grabbed her hands, so I nicely place them on top of the table instead of my lap.

"Nope, I'm from America." I look across the table and Charlotte is giving me the stink eye while Finn is just smirking. I can't help but roll my eyes at this moment. All I want to do is talk to Isla some more, maybe get her to blush another time or two, but I'm now being cockblocked by two very drunk grad students.

"Ohhh! I love Americans, ye all are so much fun. How about ye buy us a drink and we'll show ye a good time?" The blonde to her right cocks her brows up and down.

I hear a gasp from my right, and I whip my head around quickly to see a disgusted Isla staring right back at me. I'm not sure if she's disgusted by me or the girls. I look up and take a deep breath, trying to think about what to do next. Before I can tell the nice ladies I'm not interested, I feel a hand grab my cock.

"Whoa, whoa…" I grab at the hands as quickly as possible, but the drunk brunette gives me a squeeze and I can't help but groan.

"Oh my God, yer co—"

"Yer absolutely *disgusting!*" Isla screeches at both of us and pushes her chair back, she eyes the glass of whisky in front of her, and quickly grabs and throws the drink back.

"If you're going to whore yourself, why don't you take it to the back, where the toilets are, instead of doing it out here in public. What a waste of time." She slams her empty glass back down and looks at Finn and Charlotte.

"Stay, Charlotte, but I'm going to go. Thanks for the invite." She turns towards me, and I finally have both of the brunette's hands pried off of me. "Get stuffed."

She's visibly upset. I can see one of her veins on her neck pulsing, and her body is wound tight, as if it were going to snap.

"Wait, Isla…"

She's moved herself through the already busy pub and before I can chase her down, she's out the door. I run after her, hoping maybe I can reach her, but as I push the door open I see she's way too far for me to catch up.

I watch her as long as I can before she disappears. I don't like that she's walking alone this late, but I have no clue where I'm at. Finn brought me here, and I stupidly didn't pay attention. I walk through the heavy doors, back towards our table. I see Charlotte is animatedly talking to Finn, and she doesn't look happy.

"She ran out of here too fast, I wasn't able to catch her." I plop my butt down pretty hard on the chair.

"Yer unbelievable, ye know that?" Charlotte steals Finns drink and takes a gulp of it. Her face tightens and she looks like she's about to puke, but she swallows. "Disgusting."

"Babe, that was my drink." Finn grabs the bottle out of her hand and runs the back of his hand down her face.

"I know that… now! I don't know how you drink that." She scrunches up her face and quickly grabs her drink, washing the taste down with it. She points at Finn and says, "Yer distracting me," before she turns to me. "Why would ye do that?" she asks me accusingly.

"I didn't do shit. What would you have me do, knock the girl out? I didn't exactly ask her to grab me. You don't know me from Adam, but try and give me a break, Charlotte. I didn't mean to make my wildfire mad." I down the rest of my drink and look at the glass in front of me. The nice thing about attending school here is, I'm old enough to drink in this bar freely, but it also means my mouth can run away with itself.

"Your wildfire…" Charlotte's eyes are wide, and she mouths something I can't read. She cocks her head and looks at Finn, then back at me.

Shit.

Shit.

Shit. Double shit. I put my head down on the table. I didn't mean to call her *my* wildfire aloud. I look up to see Charlotte's mouth still open. I think she's about to insult me, but she just shakes her head and leans a little closer to Finn, who just keeps smiling at me.

I'm well and truly fucked. Not only do both of Isla's friends know I like her, but she absolutely hates me.

Isla

A DAY HAS GONE BY and so far my classes have been rigorous. I'm glad I've been super busy because what happened at the pub was still bothering me. Even better, I haven't had to hang around Ben, even though it looks like things are going well for Charlotte and Finn.

"Hey, I wuh-her what he's stuh-ying?" Charlotte garbles her words as she continues brushing her teeth.

"What did ye say? Why don't ye finish brushing yer teeth before sputtering whatever nonsense yer talking about."

"I was talking about Ben…" After spitting out the toothpaste, she rinses her mouth. "I wonder what he's studying. I bet ye medical because good gracious, did ye see his hands. If I weren't dating Finn, I would love to be examined by him."

"God, why are ye so crass."

"Because, Isla, someone has to be between the two of

us." She cackles and jumps on her bed. "Ye haven't said much about him since the pub."

"What's there to say, Char? He was flirting with every slutty girl in there. For goodness sake, some of them looked twice his age."

Charlotte sits up from her bed. "First off, those girls weren't twice his age. They only looked a few years older. Secondly, Isla, not everyone is a prude like you. Got to get it while it's good. And boy, is that boy… no, strike that. That *man* is hot. Like H-A-W-T, hot."

"Charlotte, ye have no morals." I laugh and grab a biscuit off my desk.

"Why, because I fancy every man I see?"

"Yes, just like that priest ye tried to tempt at church last year."

She cackles and snorts. "I bet ye he wanked off after taking my confession. Bless me, Father, for I have sinned, and all that jazz."

"Unbelievable. I cannae believe ye." I throw my pillow at her, but she catches it and hugs it.

"Isla, we are juniors and about to move towards adulthood. I guarantee yer Da will swoop ye up after ye graduate. Yer top of yer class at the business college. Every professor sings their praises of ye. If ye cannae live a little now, when will ye?"

"I get that, Charlotte, but I really don't have time."

"You'll never have time if ye don't make it." She gets up and strips out of her clothes, before tugging on her jammies.

"Don't you have class?"

"Not for a few hours. I'm going to take a nap because I'm headed down to the pub with Finn afterwards. Going to need that drink after my Statistics class. Professor Flanagan is a masochist. He likes to assign all those damn derivative assignments… I hate them."

With a yawn, Charlotte tucks herself into her blankets. I never know how she sleeps when it's this warm in the room. While I have to have something on top of me, I couldn't have a full-blown blanket covering me.

"Why are ye even minoring in Statistics if ye hate it that much?"

"Well, looks good after, right? Gotta fluff more than my professors. Plus, I got Finn now to fluff." Winking, she yawns some more, and I can't help but shake my head at her.

"I have to head to class. Do ye mind picking up a few things for me? I know ye said ye were going to Tesco later today." She nods her head. "Thanks! I left the money on the desk."

"Toodles!" She waves goodbye just before I close the door.

I walk into the classroom at least fifteen minutes early. This is the class I'd been looking forward to taking the most. It was being taught by the dean of the college, and it was an international business course. I look around and decide to sit about three rows back and in the middle. It was the best seat in the house, where I was close enough to be called on by my professor, but far enough back to see the whole room.

I start to pull out my notebook from my shoulder bag when I feel someone sit next to me. I don't bother looking up, but I wondered why, in a whole empty classroom, someone would choose to sit next to me. I keep digging in my bag, looking for my favorite pen.

Whoever is sitting next to me makes a coughing noise, but I don't look up until I've found my pen. When I sit up to place it on the desk, I startle when I see a pair of bright hazel-green eyes looking at me. It takes me a second to figure out why they're so familiar and when I pull back, I gasp. Blinking, I look around to make sure I'm in the right room, because surely, he can't be taking this class.

"You've got to be joking?"

He has the audacity to just sit there with his arms folded in front of his chest, smirking, before he pulls out an international business book. *The* international business book. The one for this class. He then pulls out a notebook and pen and places it on top of his desk.

"Why are ye even here?"

"Well, I'm studying here. Pretty haughty of you to think I'm taking this class just because you are. The universe doesn't revolve around you, Is."

"My name isn't *Is*, ye daft prick," I hiss out and try to ignore him. I can't believe he's in this class. It dawns on me that if he's in this class, he's not only a business major also, but he had to have been hand-picked to be in this program.

"I should really call you Wildfire, especially today." He reaches out and strokes the wayward hair around my face. "Red hair… even your cheeks are rosy red. I think you must like me, Wildfire."

"Whatever, yer like a venereal disease. Ye just won't go away." He grabs his stomach and laughs out loud. The people around us start to stare at us, including Professor MacNeil, who is setting up the class. I slump down in my chair a little.

"Haud yer wheesht!" I whisper, loud enough so he could hear.

"I have no idea what you just said, but it was sexy as hell."

"Yer such a bawbag," I hiss out.

"I know that one." He opens up his notebook to a page. "Do you mind repeating that other one? It really sounded like you sneezed or something."

"God, can ye be any more an eejit? Everyone is staring."

"Again, sweetheart, don't understand that one either."

"It means idiot, and I told ye to shut up. Do ye understand that one?"

"Ahhhh, my Wildfire. Never thought you'd want to be a wallflower." He leans in and gets closer to my face, and I turn because I really just want him to go away. "It's not fun standing on the sidelines."

I turn back to stare at him, but then the professor claps his hands.

"Okay, class, let us begin. I'm Professor MacNeil, and this is Advanced International Business, where we'll be looking at modern day businesses and how they've evolved over the years. All seats are final for the semester. Now, I know this will be atypical, since I'll be fitting a whole year's worth of curriculum into half, but I know all of ye can keep up. If it's too much, I implore ye to talk to Mr. Harris, who is our student aide for the class. Before we go over the curriculum, I would like ye to look to the student to yer right. They will be yer partner for the final project required of ye for this class. This project will account for twenty-five percent of yer grade."

I groan and look over at Ben, who has a wide smile on his face.

"Before I begin, I want to point out one particular student. Now, while most of ye are university students, we have a student attending from Harvard, who came highly recommended. I hear from one of my old colleagues that this would be his first time being overseas, so I would like ye all to give him a warm welcome to Scotland. Mr. Benji Dunn, if ye dinnae mind standing up."

I groan because I know his fat head won't live this down, but when I glance up, he's wincing. He quickly gives a little wave and sits down, mumbling to himself about hating that the professor did that. All I can do is glance at him. I didn't expect him to respond like that. Ben seems like a guy who relishes in accolades and praises.

"Ye must have good taste, Mr. Dunn. Miss MacDonald is one of our top students at the university. I, for one, am excited to see what ye two can come up with. Now that is out of the way, as I mentioned earlier, seat assignments cannot be switched unless dire circumstances."

I can't believe I'm stuck with this eejit. *Dobber*. Okay, maybe not stupid, he's obviously smart if he's in this class, but why, of all the students, did I get stuck with him? I don't bother looking at Ben, who I can feel staring at me throughout the class.

Every time I'm around him, I feel his presence. And not in some sort of fantasy or paranormal way I've read in the books I love, but in an unnerving way. I could feel the hairs on the back of my neck go up, and then a warmth spreading through my body.

"Okay, class dismissed. Remember the agenda that was passed out. The term paper is due in a week, and I will be administering a written exam at the end of the week, so make sure you've read the chapters ahead or you'll be out of luck."

I look up and realize I've missed the entire class, thanks to contemplating how I'd like to kill Ben in different ways. Throwing him off one of the towers would be *clean* way about it. I would think that would follow the professor's stipulation of *dire circumstances*.

"Did you even take notes?" An elbow nudges me out of my trance.

"Huh?"

"Notes, Isla. Did you even take notes?" His brows are pinched and he's staring at my blank notebook, the pen on top, with its cap still on. I can feel a burning in my cheeks as I stare at the blank page. *Oh my God, notes!*

"Ummm…"

"Here, you can take my notebook. I have another. Take down the notes and I'll get them from Finn later when he sees Charlotte." He closes his notebook and has it hovering over the desk like a gift. I can't believe I didn't take notes.

"No, that's okay—"

"Isla, don't be such a mule." He bounces the notebook in front of my face, and he has the smarmy smirk out, which puts my toes up. He looks positively delighted with himself while I'm sure mine must be flush. I fold my arms over my chest because I don't trust him. Why would he be giving me his notebook? While we may be forced to be partners, I'm still competing with him to be top of class.

His eyes turn down and a look of concern flashes. I never not take notes in any of my classes. *Never.* If anyone were to look at my previous term notebooks, you'd see them full and complete. This afterthought makes me angrier.

"I said I was fine. And did you just call me an arse?"

"No, I said don't be a mule. Two completely different things. Haven't you heard of that expression, or did your upper-class snobbery get in the way of knowing *common* tongue," he spits out.

The few times I've met Ben, he's been anything but nice to my abrasiveness, but this was a different Ben entirely. The notebook that was once slack in his hands is now held tight and his eyes are looking at me, like he wants to throw daggers.

"No, ye *dunderheid*, I haven't heard that phrase. Only fools would assume that a Scotsman or this matter, a Scotswoman, would understand an American colloquialism. Ye seem to have an aversion to my status in society. It's funny, really. The very thing ye sling at me, ye take fault in. That's not *my* problem, it's *yers*. I cannot be held accountable nor should I be made to feel ashamed about my father's wealth. He's worked hard."

This right here is the problem with men who want to mold me into what they want. They assume I'm either too stupid to understand their intentions or they want me to act a certain way.

"I will not have ye bend me into something I'm not. Like I said earlier, I didnae want to take yer stupid notes. Not everything revolves around ye, Ben. Maybe I don't need notes, did ye ever think that?" I hiss out.

Not need notes. I'm the eejit now. I'm so upset that I just start saying whatever my gob spits out, which can be dangerous. He and this class has made me so upset, I'm taking my own insecurities and placing them on him.

It's a heavy burden being the eldest daughter of *the* Craig MacDonald, and to be a business major on top of it. *A lot of pressure.* Professors and students have a lot of expectations of me. Professor MacNeil has known me since my first year. Him pointing me out was not coincidence. I've spent enough time to know he's particularly proud to have taught me, and point that out in front of the class. He does this every time I'm in one of his classes. I *hate* it. The university was excited when I chose to come here because it meant money and connections. I worked hard on my own merit—they only found out after that who my father was—but I will *always* be his daughter and not a brilliant student who worked hard.

I glare at Ben and notice most of the students have

gotten up from their desks and are leaving. A few stray behind to talk to the professor and the student assistant assigned to this class. Everyone seems too busy with their day to notice the two of us arguing with one another. *Thank God.* I take a moment to look *at* Ben instead of through him. He's stock-still, staring at his notebook like there was dung on it.

Utterly embarrassed, I can feel the heat rise. A little kind gesture and I turned it into shite. Over a stupid seat, and that he was sitting in it. I cannot bear sitting next to him the rest of term. I obviously can't control my stubbornness, and what looks to be irrationality around him.

I get up without apologizing, and leave him sitting there in the seat, because I'm an *eejit*, and ashamed is not the best word to describe that epic ridiculousness that just happened. I see an opening to talk to the professor. I can't do this with him the rest of the year, and I hope Professor MacNeil is willing to move me.

"Professor, please, if ye have a moment." I reach the bottom and he looks up, smiling at me.

"Ahhh, Isla. It's good to see yer face. I didnae see ye with yer parents a few weeks past, at the University function." He cocks his brow. I control my eye roll—I know he knows I *never* attend those functions.

"Sorry, Professor, I had prior engagements that I couldn't change. So, I don't mean to take up your time, but I was wondering if I could change my seat." I bite my lower lip and pray to Mary and Joseph he doesn't ask me why, but I know my luck in things isn't there.

"Now, Isla, ye know I can't show preferential treatment to ye just because yer father is a patron of this university. Why do ye want to move seats? Mr. Dunn is very fine student, he came highly recommended from the dean of the Economics Department at Harvard, *and* Sebastián Cardona."

"But— Wait… Sebastián Cardona of Cardona Financial?"

"The very one. Now, why a wee bonnie lass like yerself would want to turn down this opportunity. Aye, I couldn't have set it up better meself."

"But…"

"I really think both of yous could come up with a fantastic perspective. Yous from Scotland and him from America." He smiles warmly at me.

"Ummmm… I just—"

"Now I dinnae why you don't want to sit with the lad. Is it because he's good-looking? A fine-looking lad."

"What?"

"I saw yer face turning red earlier during class, and every time I saw ye staring up at him. Think of it as a cultural exchange, it's good of him to get to know Scotland." He pats my shoulder and shoos me away, like a small bairn.

Everything that's just happened seems to be going in slow motion. Did he just suggest I partake in houghmagandie? I close my mouth before he sees me gawking at him and mistakes my confusion with flirting, because it's obvious he thinks I want to shag Ben or show Ben a good time. I hear a loud slamming noise and whip around to see Ben storm off and out of the classroom.

CHAPTER *Seven*

I CAN'T BELIEVE HER. I absolutely can't believe the gall. I storm out of the classroom after watching her displaying that infantile behavior. Who acts like that? I was simply giving her my notes. I watched her staring off in space throughout the lecture. She was obviously intending to take notes, as her pen and notebook were out. And to top it off, she goes to the professor to ask to move seats. How did she think that would look? He explicitly said, *dire circumstances*. It's not like I was going to all of a sudden fall off a roof of a building.

I look down at my watch to see I have hours before my next lecture, and I can't keep standing in this building. As soon as I leave the business hall and walk out into the crisp, cool air, I take a deep breath and look around. Normally, I would ask Toby to spar with me, but he's not here to help me work off the tension. I don't know if I want to kiss her or yell at her more. Half the time, I couldn't understand what she was muttering to herself. I really need to get better at learning the language around these parts, and I'm slowly realizing the Scottish, like in America, have very distinctive accents. In my time at Harvard, I'd learned enough of the dialect in and around Massachusetts. I could point out someone from Southie immediately, and other parts of Boston, which made it easier to know if someone didn't belong in the part of Boston I was in.

I quickly head back to the dorms to change out of my jeans and into my running clothes. I'm glad I have a new pair of running shoes. The pair I had prior to flying here were falling apart and I'd been so busy, I'd forgotten to pick some up. Toby must've known I needed a pair because when I went to unpack all of my things, a brand-new pair was in my suitcase.

I look around for my small running backpack and stuff it with my water bottle, towel, spare shirt, and wallet. I make sure to grab my keys before locking up and head on out. I do a few laps around the campus area, hoping to cool off after that show with Isla, but I realize all I feel is sweaty and disgusting. She pushed all of my buttons, and I could feel the heat rise after her comment about her status in society.

Ultimately, she was right. I used my experience with rich kids against her and that wasn't her fault. It was mine. It's like she hated me on principle. All I want to do is to get to know her and she's not making it easier. I can't even scratch the surface with her, and that's most frustrating.

I slow down and jog one more lap, then decide I need to push myself more. I'm hoping something pops up on how to handle Isla going forward. I know the professor didn't grant her moving chairs. I cannot afford her completely ignoring me, because my grades depend on my *partner* being more amenable. I wander off campus and into the city. I forgot to throw in a snack and decide to pop into Tesco Express and grab myself some crisps and biscuits.

I finish the entire bag of crisps and a few biscuits before washing it down with half of my water. Breathing heavily, I look around and decide to continue on my run. I eventually pass Deaconess Garden, or at least that's what Finn called it. I pass the many unique shops that litter the city, including what looks like a gym. There are big glass windows that let me see inside, and I slow down, deciding to double back to get a closer look.

There is a small sign that just says "Gym," and I laugh to myself on how this place can even have customers. It's not distinct at all. I look around at the door to see if there were hours, since a lot of the gyms in and around Harvard stay open late. This area seems pretty decent, but I hang out in pretty slummy areas at home, so I'm not too bothered by location, as long as it has the equipment I need for working out.

A scraggly old man is at the counter up front, wearing a wife beater shirt that looks like it has seen better days. Upon closer look, I see he's got some old tracksuit pants that looked to be a decade old. He seems to be writing in some book, so I don't think he saw me come in.

"Jesus, Mary, where'd ye come from?" A loud fart rips through the room and the old man seems nonplus about it. "I almost lost me arse with ye sneaking up on an old man like that. Best that I'd not worn me whities today. The misses would've been upset if I'd made a mess of meself." He throws the pencil in the air, the one he was using to write with.

"Jesus. Too much information." I plug my nose as the old man laughs at me. He looks me over and smiles as he places his hands on his ass. I really hope he didn't shart himself. I look around and see the gym isn't anything special, but he has what I'm looking for. There are a few heavy punching bags, and the speed ones are off in the back alongside some light weight sets.

"I didn't mean to scare you. There weren't any signs outside. How much to join your gym?" I hope it isn't too much. I know Mr. Cardona gave me funds to be here, but I promised myself I wouldn't overuse anything he's given me. I don't even want to look at the account he set up for me here, because without a doubt, it was plenty. Ten times over. That was the Cardona way. They were generous to a fault, plus, I was given a business card to be used at a minimum. Emergencies, even though he said I had free rein. He even laughed at me when I asked if I could pay him back.

"Are you a boxer? Because yous kinda of scrappy-looking lad." He looks back to where my eyes are looking.

"Why do I think that?" I smile.

"I saw yous looking at them in the back." He looks me over, as if I was looking to be set up on some kind of dating service.

"No, I don't box, but I know how to fight. I use to take some hand-to-hand combat classes back at home."

"Hmmm… Home, you say. Where yous abouts? Sounds American." I smile wider at his assessment.

"I am. Studying up at the university for a bit."

"Ahhhh, American. Home of the cheeseburger. Took me wifey there, what was it, about a decade ago, for one of our anniversaries. Sure got a lot from the misses after that. If you know what I mean."

"Jesus, are you always this blunt?" I rub my forehead because I really don't want that image in my head. The old man must be well into his sixties, and no one wants to think about someone as old as their grandpa having sex.

"Of course, laddie! Never hide nothing, is what I always say. Best to be honest than lie." He winks and comes around the front desk. "So, what say yous, standing out there. Were ye looking to join?"

"I was just going for a run and I miss working out a bit. I didn't see any signs on pricing." I look around for more any indication of how much it costs to join. The old man is peculiar, but nice.

"Signs… No signs, but if yous looking to join, there is a monthly fee of twenty-six pounds. But a onetime fee of twenty pounds to cover the heres and theres. Towels and water are covered."

I quickly try to calculate what this means. Pounds to dollars still confused the hell out of me. Unexpectedly, despite being good with numbers, carrying coins is really confusing. Anywhere from one pence to two, and don't get me started on the pound coin and two-pound coin. Finn constantly laughs when I go to pay for anything. Usually, I pull out a handful of coins and push them around my palm. If I have to contend with Isla the rest of the semester, I'm really going to need this.

"Okay, I think that'll work." I pull my bag off and grab my wallet, handing him the twenty pounds and a few months ahead.

"Ahhh, lad, this is too much."

"If you don't mind putting me down for a few months, I don't always carry this much on me." I throw my wallet back into my bag. I look around and see the time; I still have plenty before my next class. "Is it okay to work out now?"

"Aye, go on, lad. Don't let me bother you." He smiles and looks down at his notebook. I can see a bunch of numbers and realize it looks like it's a handwritten accounting system. He closes the book with a wince, and from his expression, I wonder if he's fallen on hard times. I walk over and place the bag in the little cubbies along the wall. There isn't anyone in here, so I think I can safely leave it there while I work out.

"So, what ye studying at the university? Must be smart," the old man shouts over by the desk.

"Why'd you say that? I could be dumber than a rock." He tilts his head, perplexed by the expression, but doesn't say anything.

"I cannae imagine University taking a lad like ye if ye were 'dumber than a rock.' They'd look like a bunch of arses." He laughs so hard you'd think the ceiling would cave in. Again, looking around, I wonder how safe this building is.

"I'm studying business, but my focus is more on international business. There are a few adjunct professors at the university I really want to learn from."

"Don't know what adjunct means, but like I said, smart. I've never been good with numbers meself. Take me right now, can't even balance my books. Me wife helps out, but she's been helping me daughter out the last few weeks." He thumps at the notebook.

I look over to where he's standing. "I could always look them over if you want? What seems to be the problem?"

He eyes me warily. "Ah, lad, ah dinnae ken. Don't worry about it, I'll figure it out. I'm just talking out me arse. My wife says I talk too much, but I cannae help it. I like to talk!"

I just shake my head. Maybe he'll let me help him out later, after he warms up to me.

"Do you have any tape I can use? I don't mind paying for it."

"Aye, look over in that top cabinet, there should be one. Like I said, the monthly charge covers it. Do ye need help taping?"

"If you don't mind." I smile widely at him and he strolls on over. He seems more than happy to help.

"Yous shouldn't do it on your own. I used to box, ye know? I was Edinburgh's middle weight champion. I'm auld now but not auld enough to teach you a round or two, lad." He grabs my hand and begins to expertly tape my hands up so I can hit the bags.

"So, show me what you got!"

He steps back and we go several rounds, trying to get into the rhythm, which doesn't take long since I'm still amped up from earlier. I wish I could get her out of my head. She's a pain in the ass but I still want her. My brain is telling me to run away from her. She's too much. Uncontrollable. But do I want to control her? I know she's afraid, I can hear it her voice. *Expectation.* I would imagine, being who she is, people expect a lot from her. As much as I hate my roots being thrown at me—I'm a poor kid from Lancaster in a fancy school—but what must it be like to be rich? Everyone wants something from you. Molding you into something you don't want. It must be repressive.

No, Isla isn't the kind of gal who should be kept. My nickname does her justice. But, she's too hot and I know she'll burn me. I'm only here for a short while, but tell my heart that. It wants her, more than anything I've ever wanted before. I grew up trying to not want too much, because life has a way of kicking you in the face. I was a half-empty-glass kind of guy, but as I grew older, I knew I couldn't continue to think the other shoe was going to drop. I had to dream bigger, to be better. Could Isla be my other half? Someone to help push me. A partner who I could lean on during the bad times. A partner who made me a better person.

I keep hitting and hitting at the bag until my arms begin to burn. I finally slow down and lean into the bag, hugging it to hopefully calm down my heart. I was so focused, I forgot the old man was watching me.

"So, what has ye in a tizzy?" He has his arms folded across his chest, making his biceps more prominent. I can see he must've been in really good shape at some point in time.

"Nothing, I just like to punch." I wince, because even that sounds lame.

"Bullocks, something is bothering ye. I can tell, lad. I've spent years training boxers and I've seen what it looks like to be frustrated. Let me guess. A lass?" He cocks his brow.

"How did you—"

"How did I know it was about a lass? Laddie, it's *always* about that." He smiles. "So, tell me about her."

"She's... She's..." I take a deep breath. "I don't know, she's just, something about her just makes me want things." He gestures for me to keep going. I know I'm not giving him much help.

"What's she like? Obviously, ye like the lass. Is she bonnie?"

"What does that mean? I hear everyone use that word, but I don't want to sound stupid." He tosses me a bottle of water, which I down about half.

"Ahhhh, bonnie. Well, when describing a lass, it means pretty, but more beautiful." He hands me a spray to help him clean up after myself, and I suspect giving me time to get my words right.

"Isla is gorgeous. Beautiful blue eyes and bright red hair. I've never seen anything more stunning." The old man stops what he's doing and smiles wide at me.

"I hear a but here somewhere..."

I rub my forehead and toss the paper towel I'd been using to wipe down the bag. "Yeah, she hates me and I don't know how to change it."

"Ahhhh, laddie, me wifey hated me too, the first time I'd met her. Headstrong woman, but lovely as the day I'd seen her. Many Scottish women are like that. They have to be to deal with bastards like us." He laughs so hard he has tears in his eyes.

"How'd you get her to like you?"

"Persistence and patience. I wore her down. If she's stubborn, yous need to wear her down. And show her yer heart. What's inside here"—he points at my chest, then down—"and not down there. A beautiful lass like you describe needs more than a good nob, you sees. Be patient with her and she'll come around. I can tell, yous a nice lad. Nine out of ten I find women act cold because of fear. So, show her the good."

He slaps me hard on my back. "She'll comes around when she does, promise ye that, laddie."

We talk more about his wife and he goes on and on about their life together. By the end, she sounds just like Isla, if not more stubborn. I'm glad I decided to stop in here. I really need a place to let off steam, and I'm fairly certain this old man was placed on my path for reason.

CHAPTER *eight*

ISLA

CLASSES GO BY WITHOUT INCIDENT with Ben. Despite having classes together, we haven't had a row since that last time in Professor MacNeil's class. No matter the setting, everything seemed *too* cordial. From the short time I'd spent with Ben, he was anything but distant. Now that he is, I should be happy about it, but I'm not. All I seem to get out of him are monosyllabic responses.

I think about the few times I'd met him, and I wonder what about him made me feel indifferent to him. I couldn't even answer that question, despite asking myself all the time. And that made feel ashamed. I couldn't have been more visceral in my attempts to cut him down. He's a foreigner in my country, who seemed generally interested to getting to know me. I should have been more hospitable. There are things I can't take back now. I *knew* better.

A piece of popcorn gets flung in my face, bringing me

out of my daze. I'd been sitting at my desk, trying to decide how to start my paper for one of my classes.

"Hey, what's that for?" I glance over at Charlotte, who's eating a bowl of fresh made popcorn, busy flipping through a fashion magazine instead of studying, like she said she should be doing.

"Seriously, Isla, what is wrong with ye? You've been sitting there for ten minutes, not saying a word, even though I thought ye were listening."

"Oh…" I bite my lower lip and put down the pencil I had grasped in my hand.

"Yeah, oh… So, what seems to be the problem? Ye don't normally have such a difficult time starting yer papers." She pops a handful of popcorn in her mouth and chews. Despite Charlotte going to boarding school her whole life, you'd think she would have better manners, but sometimes she eats like a pig.

"How do ye know that?"

"Mergawd, I known ye long enough." She tries to quickly chew down her food but manages to spit some out in her attempts.

"Seriously, yer so rank." She smiles wide, with popcorn kernels sticking in her teeth. I point at her face. "Case in point."

She doesn't even have the decency to apologize, just washes her mouth out with a bottle of Irn Bru. She smacks her lips and continues to shove more popcorn in.

"No more delay tactics, my dear friend, I know what yer doing. I happen to enjoy popcorn; it tastes best right out of the oven." She waves her hand around, gesturing for me to continue.

"I was just thinking—"

What do I tell her? I can't exactly tell her I was thinking about Ben. She's dating his roommate, so I don't particularly want to get it back to him. He's already got a fat head about things. We have been competing for top grade in class. While the students in my university are smart, I work hard to keep my grades the highest. It's not just an ego thing, but I want the best opportunity to work where I want. While working for my Da's company would be appealing and to some extent, *easier*, I don't want easy. I want a challenge, where I can stand on my own two feet. I don't want life to always be handed to me, nor do I expect it.

"I was just thinking about class," I lie, and an easy one that would be believable, since Charlotte knows I'm a perfectionist. She makes a loud buzzing sound like I gave her the incorrect answer. *Okay, maybe not.*

"Try again."

"I—"

Charlotte cocks her brow and folds her arms across her chest. "Think long and hard before ye lie to me again, Isla Sophie MacDonald, or I'll thrash ye about. Ye *never* lie to me, dinnae why yer starting now… unless it's about a boy." She smirks.

I'm stunned, not sure what to say. If I look at her, she'll know she's right, and I *hate* when she's right because she'll make a spectacle of it.

"I—"

"I'll help ye out. Could it be about a boy ye mouthed off to… maybe during a particular classroom encounter." She shakes her head and smirks at me before popping a few pieces of popcorn in her mouth.

"How did ye know?" I shift in my seat and wonder how much she's been told. Charlotte just rolls her eyes. I pause and stare at her and it dawns on me she's seeing Finn. "How much did he tell ye?"

"He didnae have to. He came storming into their room that day you must've had a row with him. His fists were slightly swollen, and he was drenched right through his shirt. Finn asked him if he was okay, and he just cursed out your name, but shut his gob when he realized I was in the room."

"So, Finn just outright told you about what happened?" Charlotte had the audacity to laugh at my question.

"Not at first, but I have my ways." She smirks and I narrow my eyes, hoping she understands it's not good to tease because his behavior now is just peculiar.

"I think ye hurt his feelings, Isla. Yer too in yer head sometimes, and for a boy like Ben, yer abrasiveness put him off. I dinnae why yer putting up a fight with him when he's just being nice."

"He's not nice."

Charlotte aimlessly throws her pillow at me, hitting me in the face, when I know she was probably aiming it somewhere else.

"Hey, that hurt!" I throw the pillow back at her, but miss, and it falls to the ground next to the foot of her bed.

"Hey you, now who isn't the nice one. It's not like ye to be this *mean*."

"I—"

"And don't start. We both know ye started it with him, not the other way around. Ye should be ashamed with yerself. Ye put up these walls so no one can like ye for *you*. Automatically thinking someone wants something from ye, or expects ye to be someone else. *Maybe* if ye took the time to get to know someone, ye might actually find someone doesn't have ulterior motives. Did ye ever think about that?" Charlotte gets up and grabs a few things, throwing them in her bag.

"Ye need to make this right, Isla, I really mean it. Not just because he's Finn's roommate, but he's a nice guy. Get to know him first. Maybe you'll find he's not who ye think he is."

"What does that mean? Did he say something to ye?"

"Not my place to tell ye." She loops her bag over her shoulder and turns to leave.

"Hey, whose side are ye on?"

Turning slightly, her mouth downturns and she blinks rapidly. "Always on yer side, remember that."

She opens the door and walks out, leaving me to silently sit at my desk with only my thoughts. My best friend just verbally slapped me into seeing how wrong I was. What did she mean when she said it wasn't her place to tell? Isn't that what besties are supposed to do. *Tell* each other secrets. Why is she holding on to what Ben has or hasn't said to her?

Groaning, I look out the window and open it up to get some fresh air. A cool, crisp breeze flows into the room and I take a deep breath. I can't just stay in here, locked up in my room. It's still early and I can take a stroll around the campus. I grab my bag and a light coat to wear, just in case it gets too cold.

This time of year is usually my favorite season. We are getting into cooler temperatures, which means I can pull out my cuter jumpers. I swing by George Square instead of the Meadows because the walk was going to be too long. I think back to my first encounter with Ben—the look he gave me when I was yelling at his stupid throw wasn't of contempt. It was amusement. Most of the guys on the team have seen my fair share of blowouts after a loss. I was an avid rugby fan, like the rest of my family. I've gotten into loads of heated arguments with some of the players. Ben could've hated me on principle but during class, he was anything but. He offered me notes, when most of the students in the class would have shunned me if I asked to borrow theirs. Why would he do that? Surely it wasn't just out of politeness? The looks he has given me… I shake my head because there is *no way* that—

"Hey, Isla, wait up! Didn't ye hear me shouting yer name?"

I turn around to see Peter Umbridge running towards me. He's wearing a tweed coat, and smart trousers. Notably I see he's gotten a new pair of glasses. I've known Peter since primary school seven. His family relocated to Scotland from London, where he spent most of his primary years, so when he arrived, there were a bit of learning pains on his part. He had no friends initially, and I was different then, more open and inclusive. I had asked him to sit with the group of kids I hung out with, and ever since then, he seemed keen on me.

He was always that boy who wanted to share lunches and play on the playground with me, but despite him being a nice guy, I've never felt a connection with him. Or maybe I just haven't given him a chance, like Charlotte suggested. I *never* give guys a chance, I've been burned one too many times.

"Oh sorry, Peter, just got a lot on my mind."

He slows down and lifts his arms up for a hug, which I oblige. His arms wrap around me tightly and he holds on a little longer than normal before pulling back and kissing my cheek lightly, which catches me a bit off guard. I pull back a little and I think that startled him. His brow pulls forward.

"I didn't mean to frighten ye. It's just a friendly kiss. Unless, ye might want to go out on a date with me, so that kiss can mean more?"

Oh my God, did he just say that? *Awkward.* He looks at me intently, as if awaiting my answer.

"Oh, Peter—"

"Forget it, Isla. It's fine. I mean, ye *never* agree, even

when I ask. I get it." He scuffs his shoes against the sidewalk.

"No, look, I dinnae what to say. I've known ye for a long time, Peter. It just might be awkward. I'm not very nice," I spit out, because if I were honest with myself, I really am too abrasive. If Ben is a good example, I'm downright mean.

"Isla…"

"I really am, Peter. I don't know why you'd want to go out with me. I'm rude—"

"You've never been rude to me, Isla, you've been lovely as can be. It doesn't have to be serious. We can go for coffee, or even a drink at one of the pubs ye fancy?" He smiles expectantly.

Before I can answer him, as we're cutting through the park, I see a bunch of girls surround a guy with no shirt on. I roll my eyes, but as I take a closer look, I see it's not just any guy, it's Ben.

"I can't believe those girls are just throwing themselves at him," I mutter.

"Who?" Peter gazes over to where I'm looking. "That guy? What a tosser, it's ten degrees out." Even from afar, I can see the sweat glistening off his hard body. He's smiling down at them, not stopping them from touching his chest, which upsets me more than I care to admit. Something warm bubbles inside of me and I can't explain my reaction.

"Isla, did you hear me?" Peter snaps his fingers in front of my face and leans in a little closer. I instantly take a step back at his closeness.

"No sorry, just distracted."

"Ye like that?"

"*What*?!"

"Him. Ye like him?" I turn my gaze away from Ben and the slutty girls towards Peter. His cheeks are slightly redder than before and he looks upset about something. He looks down at me and back at Ben.

"Oh God, no! He's too arrogant. He's my class partner for the International Business class I'm taking." I roll my eyes. "Just an obnoxious American with no manners."

I wave my hands in the air but my gaze looks back towards Ben, who's now looking my way. My eyes lock on his and his cold, hard eyes stare back at me. His mouth thins as Peter moves a little closer to me. The maneuver blocks my view, but I can still see Ben's hands, which are now clenched at his side.

"Isla, come have coffee with me? Or something. Seriously, no pressure." Peter snaps his fingers again to get my attention. If I wasn't so focused on what was happening across the way, I would've told Peter off for snapping at me, like I was some kind of dog.

Peter shifts again and I see Ben smirk at me, then swing his arm around one of the girls surrounding him, which just takes the piss out of me. I feel a heat making its way up my neck and face. Something about the gesture feels like I'm playing some kind of cat-and-mouse chase, and I just lost. I absolutely refuse to get upset over this, yet I can't help but feel a tightness in my chest. I look up at Peter, who is waiting for my answer.

"Okay."

CHAPTER *nine*

Ben

"**F**UCK," I SPIT OUT.

"What's wrong?" One of the random girls, I think she said her name was Amelia, is looking at me with her doe eyes.

"Nothing, I'm sorry." I remove my arm from her shoulder.

My natural disposition can come off charming and flirtatious, and normally, I'm not forward like that with a girl I just met. But when I saw Isla with that guy, it felt like a stab in the gut, even though I had no right to feel like that. She still hated me. After talking to Old Man Ferguson, I thought giving Isla some time was the best thing. She'd been cordial in class, and I hoped she didn't become indifferent with me.

I don't know what is worse, indifference or hatred. After talking to Finn, we both concluded hatred was the better route. Indifference is pretending like that person doesn't exist, like they mean nothing, while hatred is an emotion I could work with, because no one would spend that amount of time and energy if they cared. Like Finn said, I just needed to get past that hard exterior she's built up.

I want time to get to know her, and I'm running out of what precious time I have left in Scotland. The girls didn't help. My intention wasn't to have them surround me while on my run, so when I got waved down and slowed to see what they wanted, I didn't think they would immediately start to flirt and touch me. I happened to look up after I tried to remove Amelia's hands from my chest and saw Isla. Her red hair was unmistakable.

Seeing Isla with that guy just pissed me off. I know I'm jumping to conclusions, and if I could lip read, I would've tried. My logic dictates this wasn't an innocent conversation. The douchebag was inching closer and closer to her. I saw her step back a few times, but didn't stop his unwarranted leanings.

On impulse, just to piss her off, I threw my arm over Amelia without putting two thoughts to what I was doing. If she can flirt with this guy, then so could I. It's not a nice thing to tease Amelia into thinking she has a chance, but it's not like I promised her a date or forever. I know that makes me an ass. I know it, and Isla knows it. The look on her face could only be described as heartbreaking. I never want to hurt her, and yet, I did. I wonder why I feel like I *always* have to take it to this level with her? I know Old Man Ferguson would've smacked me around in the ring if he knew I did that. He's been going on and on about how I should show her my heart and instead, I show her my ass. Or, as he says, *arse*.

I keep replaying what happened just a moment ago, I didn't even hear Amelia or any of her friends talking to me.

"Ben, we have to go, but if yer ever need of company,

give me a ring." She quickly shoves a piece of paper in my hand and smiles up at me.

I don't answer her and just watch the girls walk away. I open my hand up to see she'd written her number down. My gut feels like it bottomed out. I used this virtual stranger to get back at the girl I really like. A girl who truly loathes me. A girl who refuses to talk to me more than a few seconds. I'm dirt beneath her shoes.

Isla's hurt face flashes back at me. Her *hurt* face. Hurt isn't hatred, but something else entirely. I spent this whole time nudging her along, like poking at an angry bear to get a reaction. Isla has only been angry at me, but this is different. As much as I hate myself for using Amelia, I got more information about Isla. She was *jealous*.

People don't get hurt when someone they know hates them. Quite the opposite. Isla's reaction gives me hope I can win her over, but I fucked up royally and now, I don't know how to fix things.

CHAPTER *ten*

Skirt and cute top. *No*. Dress. *Absolute no*. I seriously have nothing to wear. Okay, strike that. I have clothes to wear, but what does one wear to a non-date, date? I don't want Peter to get the wrong impression. I already feel a bit guilty saying yes, but he was being so nice about it and he *did* say it was a no-pressure date.

Watching Ben with those slutty girls put me on my toes. I know I have no right to be upset, but I was. It felt like something hit me in the pit of my stomach and squeezed at my heart. I've never felt anything like that before and it scared me. It wasn't hate, or indifference. *I knew that much.* I keep putting off what I think it is, hoping the feeling would just go away on its own, but I've spent a few days waking up restless. Admitting it in my heart, or even aloud, would mean I would have to face everything head-on. Despite being right most times, I don't know how to fix this.

"Are ye going out?"

"Huh?" I have a blouse I'd been looking at grasped tightly in my hands.

"You've been staring at yer closet for ten minutes, Isla. I've never seen ye care about what yer wearing. If ye want my opinion, it's a little warm out. If yer going with a dress, I'd wear something a little shorter, but I really like that blouse."

She brushes out her long brown hair I've always been jealous of. Being the *only* redheaded MacDonald is bad enough—my Da says one of his great-great aunts had also been a redhead—but it's always made me stand out in a way I didn't particularly like. Redheads were notoriously known for being hotheads, and my personality didn't help with those stereotypes.

"Ugh, I dinnae what to wear." I turn towards Charlotte and lean against my closet door. "What do ye wear to a non-date, date?"

Charlotte's eyes lit up. "Ohhhhh, did Ben finally ask ye out?"

"What?" I narrow my eyes. "What did you just say?"

"Ben mentioned to Finn he was thinking of asking ye out, but he'd acted like a complete *arse* the last time he'd seen ye. Please, *please*, tell me ye said yes."

She claps her hands and does a little wiggly butt dance.

"Charlotte…" I bite my lip, because I don't know what to say to that. Ben asking me out would be the very absolute last thing I'd expect he'd do. Call me out in front of class to humiliate me, yes. But a date? Never. It would mean he's liked me this whole time.

"And, Isla, I dinnae think he would think this is a non-date, date. That boy is totally smitten with ye."

My mouth drops open and I slowly take in what she's just told me. Ben likes me. And not to tease, not for fun.

He's told his roommate and mine that he likes me. What. The. Fuck.

"What's wrong?" There's a certain sort of uncertainty in the tone of her voice as she stops mid-brush. Her eyes narrow and she finally puts her brush down, waiting for me to respond.

"It's not Ben." I lower my gaze to my feet, staring at the socks I've put on, and wonder if it's acceptable to go on a date wearing bright unicorn socks.

"If it's not Ben, then who is it?" Her voice hitches, the excitement from earlier seeming to wane.

"Ummm… Peter Umbridge." I refuse to look at Charlotte, so I quickly grab a pair of pants from the closet. Blouse and sensible pants will have to do.

"Peter Umbridge!" Charlotte squeaks out. "I *hate* him, Isla. Why, on all the hills of Scotland, would ye say yes to *him*? That boy is horrid. He snaps at ye like a dog. He has no respect—"

"Peter is very nice. He was really polite asking me out." I unbutton the blouse, so I can swap it with the ratty pajama top I have on.

"Isla, dates aren't supposed to be *nice*. They are meant to be unrelenting. Hot. Do ye even like him, or did ye say yes out of spite?" Her voice hitches up several more octaves.

While lying would be preferable, she's right. I said yes when normally, I would've turned him down, like I have time and time again. I don't feel anything but familiarity when around Peter. There's no lust. No heat when I'm around him. It's quite the opposite of when I'm around Ben.

"Can't ye just tell him yer not feeling well. I *know* ye, Isla. This is a mistake." She stomps her feet on the floor and places her hands on her hips to prove a point.

"Ye know I cannae do that. It would be improper. He'll

know I'm ghosting him. It's innocent. Like I said earlier, non-date… date." I quickly strip out of my comfy loungewear and into the pants and blouse. I finish brushing my hair out while ignoring Charlotte, who is still standing there, huffing about.

"Isla, fine. Get this out of yer system. Peter is a *bore*. Promise me something though. If Ben asks ye out, like legit asks ye out, dinnae turn him down. Dinnae be snide or rude about it…"

"I—"

Charlotte grabs me by the shoulders and rolls her eyes. "Ye would, but please. Go on a date with him, get to know him. You'll be surprised what he's like once ye let him climb that wall you've built in front of ye. I've told ye this before. Not everyone wants something of ye. Not everyone wants to change ye." She kisses me on the cheek lightly and gives me a hug before wandering back to her desk to finish brushing out her hair.

At half past seven, a knock sounds at the door. I've been ready for the last half hour, going over everything Charlotte had told me. Maybe I mistook his intentions. While Ben can give as good as he gets, I know virtually nothing about him. My head wants to stay away but my heart is thinking otherwise.

Charlotte gets up to grab the door. "Hello, Peter."

"Charlotte." Peter's voice sounds downturn and slightly cold.

"Ugh, yer so annoying. Hold on, let me get her. Isla, that boy is here." She walks back towards me as I make my way to the door. "Isla, if it's a terrible date, call me. I'll come get ye out of it," she whispers, and squeezes my arm lightly.

When I open the door, Peter is waiting patiently for me. He's wearing a pair of trousers that looks like something my

Da would wear, and a tweed coat. I control my need to roll my eyes. Peter is the same age as me, but dresses much older than anyone our age would.

"Hey, Peter, thanks for picking me up here." I smile politely but stay somewhat at a distance. After Charlotte's revelation, something about getting *too* close to Peter and giving him the wrong impression seemed wrong.

"Ye look very pretty, Isla." He steps forward to either give me a hug or a kiss on the cheek, but I side-step to the right and he's able to half-hug me. His brow pulls forward, but he doesn't say anything about the slight. "So, there's a decent pub up the way. We can walk if that works?"

"Sure, that sounds nice." I smile again because what else am I supposed to do? We both walk side by side, talking about our classes. Everything seems very casual as we stroll along the streets of Edinburgh. The city has dimmed a bit, but there is plenty of lighting on the streets, giving the city a warm glow. Our conversation slows as we get closer to the pub, and things grow a bit awkward.

"Here we are. It looks a bit crowded. Did ye want to go somewhere else?" There seems to be pockets of people loitering outside, and it's hard to push through the doors. I don't really fancy walking anywhere else.

"No, this will work. Let's try in the back and see if there's a table." Peter shuffles me inside. The crowds don't make it easy for personal space, and he places his hand on my back. I look around quickly to see if there are any chairs. When I turn, I see a pair of familiar eyes staring at me from the far-end table. *Ben.* At first, he looks surprised, but then he frowns and there is a hint of sadness in his stare.

Shite. In that moment, I'd just like to redo today and crawl in a hole. I wish he didn't see me with Peter. A feeling a dread washes over me as we move further into the back.

Despite how dark it is in the pub, I can see a reddish glow grow on Peter's cheeks as he looks down at me. He turns his head slightly and looks back at the table I'd been staring at. *Double shite*. I know he sees Ben sitting on the other side of the room. Peter grabs my arms and pulls me forward. His grip is harder than normal, and I wince.

"Peter," I breathe out. He doesn't say a word, but continues to hold my arm in place. I try to pull away, but he doesn't let go until we're seated at the small empty table. I sit down and rub where he'd been holding me, hoping he wasn't intentionally trying to hurt me. It's not something I thought Peter would do, and when I look up at him sitting across from me, he has a gentle smile on his face. Maybe he was just making sure we got to our table before someone stole it.

"Phew, I didn't think we would get past that crowd of people." Okay, so maybe it was just *that*, since he doesn't bring up the fact I'd been staring at Ben.

I laugh nervously. "Yeah, it's a bit crowded, but this place looks right nice."

"I've been here a few times. They have a good selection of beer and whisky. Now that we're seated, let me grab our drinks. Ye drink whisky, right?"

"Yeah, I like Macallan, but maybe I can get a glass of wine instead. Just have the bartender recommend. I prefer red but if they don't have it, a dry white wine works too."

"No problem, I'll be right back." He smiles and leaves me to myself. I know wine gets me drunk faster, but I really don't feel like drinking whisky tonight. From here, I can't see Ben and that gives me some peace of mind. If he was looking to ask me out, I don't think it's good to have him watching me on my "date." Peter comes back quickly with our drinks. Instead of a glass of wine, he's carrying a bottle back to the table with an empty glass.

"Peter, I won't be able to drink all of that by myself," I gasp, because buying a bottle would be such a waste.

"It's no worries, much cheaper by the bottle. You'll like this one, he says it's a popular French wine." He places the opened bottle in front of me and the empty glass. "Give it a second to breathe, I'll be right back. I have to grab my drink."

He leans in and before I get a chance to realize what he's about to do, he kisses me softly on my cheek, pausing a bit longer than normal before pulling back. He looks at me heatedly, and it's a look that doesn't make me feel any better being on this date with him. I must've been holding my breath, because I let it out as soon as he moves away from the table, back towards the bar.

Thankfully, he doesn't try anything like that again, and we spend the rest of the night talking about our families to pass the time. Peter has been polite and helped me to relax throughout the evening. By the time we are ready to go, I've finished the entire bottle of wine by myself.

"Oh dear, I'll be right back. I've got to stop off at the ladies' room before we head back."

Peter's eyes glaze over a moment and he nods. I look down at our table, and there are at least five empty glasses on the table. We are both smashed.

I wobble my way to the other side of the bar, where the toilets are. I stumble for a moment, but before I fall and hit the floor, strong arms stop me.

I giggle, looking down at the shoes of the gentleman who helped me out. I grab hold of his forearms to help steady myself. When the floor isn't swaying anymore, I look up and gasp. Ben is standing in front of me with a frown.

"Hello, Wildfire," he says with a heady voice, though there is a mark of concern in his tone.

"Oh… Umm… Hi." I smile and hold onto him a little

tighter. I feel a little lightheaded and I really do need to pee, but something about being in his presence while I'm like this makes me stop.

"Are you okay?" His voice wavers a little.

"I've got to pee. But—"

"But?"

"But this feels nice too. Thanks for catching me," I say softly, unsure what else to say.

"You're welcome. I'll always catch you, Wildfire."

I don't know what's wrong with me, but I can feel burning behind my eyes. I really shouldn't have had this much wine. I don't know what Peter was playing at by getting us both this drunk. He said it was innocent. Ben pulls me into a hug and I return the embrace. In that moment, a sense of warmth washes over me.

"Don't go home with him," he says softly into my hair. I shake my head, not sure what to say. My intentions were never to go home with Peter. Everything is so confusing right now. Mixed emotions and alcohol together don't do well with me. I squeeze him a little harder.

"I really have to pee."

He pulls back and lifts my chin up to see my face. My lip trembles as his gaze softens. For a moment, I think he's going to lean and kiss me, but he pulls away from me and nods.

I quickly rush into the bathroom and into one of the empty stalls, where I sit and fall apart. I can feel the blood rush to my face as I flush a short while later. I can't be in here much longer or I'm going to make it even more awkward. I finish up in the bathroom and look at one of the mirrors. My face is a little puffy from the tears that have fallen. I turn on the water and rinse my face off with some cold water, hoping the redness will subside. I dry up, realizing this is as good as it's going to get. I pray Ben isn't just waiting outside for me because I really don't fancy a fight between Ben and Peter on who is going to take me home. I know Ben would beat Peter to a pulp if provoked.

When I step out, Ben isn't waiting for me, and I don't bother looking for him because I really can't handle him while I've taken this much drink. I walk back to our table and see Peter waiting impatiently.

"Hey, sorry, do ye mind if we duck out now?"

His gaze moves up to my face and his mouth thins, but he doesn't say anything else. We both walk out without incident. I do wobble around on my feet, but Peter doesn't bother to help me along like he did before, which then reminds me of Ben and his comment earlier, about always being there to catch me.

As soon as we walk into the night air, I take a deep breath and sigh. I'd been getting a tad bit warm in the bar —part of it was the amount of wine I'd just had, but also being this close to Ben after everything makes me feel things. Things I'm not quite ready to address.

Peter and I silently walk down the street, which seems to be empty at the moment. I was too inebriated to notice how abnormal things were. I surely wasn't paying attention to what road we were going down. When I snap out of my thoughts, it appears Peter seems to be cutting us through an area with less traffic. I trip over my feet a little, and I get grabbed hard again. Before I know it, I'm pulled back and hard lips are on mine. My brain is slow to move on what is happening. These lips are not the ones I want on me as I open my eyes wide.

Peter has me in his rigid grip, and it's not comfortable at all. I squirm and try to get him to release me, but he pulls me in closer. He has me so tight, and I can feel him getting harder the longer he has me in his grasp. He groans and slightly lessens his grasp, which allows me to step back and slap him in the face.

"Peter, ye had no right!" I scream and slap him in the face a second time. The moment I do, I know I made a mistake. His fists are taut.

"Ye bitch!" He moves towards me and I take a few steps before he can get close enough to grab me.

I turn to run, but before I can get away, he grabs hold of my hair that'd been flowing in the wind and pulls hard. My head snaps back and I pull forward as hard as I can, but I can't get him to let go. I'm trapped. I try to scream, but he's now got his hand covering my mouth so tightly I can't even bite him. He pushes me against a wall, my face scraping the sharp stone, and I feel a sting along my cheek. Turning me around, he steps back enough to swing his hand forward and slap me hard. A burst of pain hits my eyes. Tears fall, and before I can lift my head, I feel him ripping at my blouse, then gripping my breast hard.

"I'll make you pay for that. I'll ruin you, Isla. No one is going to want you, not even that *dunderheid*. Especially after I have my way with you," he spits out. "Yer such a cocktease, and I'm tired of ye playing games."

I can smell the stink of alcohol on his breath. I try and scratch his face, but he easily slaps my hands away. I cry out as he opens my blouse wider. I try to cover myself with my trembling hands, but he pulls on my arm, so hard I think he's going to break it. I panic and scream, praying I can get him to stop. I close my eyes, because I can't bear to accept what's about to happen.

Taking a deep breath, I scream one last time, in hopes someone can hear me, but I know the chances are slim. Peter has pulled me into some kind of abandoned alleyway. I cringe and cry out when he squeezes me harder. Then, suddenly, the pain stops.

I crack open my eyes and see someone has Peter in a contorted body lock, so hard he cries out in pain. I can't see who it is because it's so dark. I should run, but everything is hurting, and I collapse onto the ground. I watch as Peter tries to pull back and hit whoever is trying to help me out. But the man is too quick and he dodges Peter's pathetic punch. The man throws not one, but four or five punches. Before Peter can fall to the ground, he's grabbed by his shirt and the stranger punches several more times.

I hear the crunch of bones breaking, and blood is flowing down Peter's unconscious face. Whoever is hitting him seems determined to *kill* him. I groan because a sharp pain hits me in the side. The man glances my way, then drops Peter to the ground and rushes over to me. I've tumbled forward, wincing at the pain.

"Isla—" An anguished voice I recognize calls out my name. It's impossible, I don't know how he could be here.

"Ben," I sob, and shake uncontrollably.

CHAPTER *eleven*

WHEN I WENT OUT TONIGHT, my intentions weren't to run into Isla. I needed to have a moment of calm. For weeks, I'd been talking to Finn and Charlotte about her. Probably excessively so, to the point where Charlotte threatened to tell Isla herself if I didn't grab my balls and ask her out. I was just trying to figure out how to do it. There is no way Isla would've had any clues I liked her, not with my behavior. We fought like cat and mouse, so much so, it was hard to figure out who was the cat and who was the mouse.

So, I was shocked to see Isla walk into the pub I was in. Except, she wasn't alone, but with that douchecanoe. The preppy one I saw earlier. I can't imagine Charlotte telling me to ask Isla out if she were dating this guy. I've heard Charlotte tell Finn she'd cut off his *bawbag* if she ever caught him flirting with any other girls, so I knew Charlotte wasn't the kind of woman who would recommend her friend if she were dating someone.

I tried ignoring Isla and *that* guy, but I'd catch glances here and there throughout the night. That idiot had bought her a bottle of wine, which she seemed to be downing at an uncomfortable rate. I saw neither of them eating food along with their drinks, and that made me nervous.

By happenstance, when I went to stop at the bathroom, so was she, and I could immediately tell she was incredibly uncoordinated. I couldn't help myself and show her how I felt in that moment. I was concerned, and didn't want to scare her away by telling her not to go with him. I didn't trust him at all. Who gets a girl *that* drunk? Instead of letting her go home unguided, I took a chance and told her not do it.

What I didn't expect her to do was to hug me back, and not in a polite way, but out of trust. I wanted to scoop her up and take her out of there, but she said she had to pee. My first mistake was letting her go. My second was not being there when she came out.

I myself had to use the restroom, but the men's room was packed. I had to wait my turn and by the time I got out, I panicked. I briskly walked back towards where her table was, but she was gone and so was the guy.

I ran out of the bar and took a chance, heading down-hill towards where I thought they might've gone to. While scrambling down, worried I was going along the wrong path, I heard a muffled scream reverberate somewhere close by. I stopped and listened closely, to see if I could hear the noise again, but nothing came. I walked slowly to peek around, to see if they decide to cut through one of the alleyways. I heard another scream but this time, much louder, and I knew something was wrong. I followed the noise to where I thought it had come from.

When I ran through the alleyway, I could barely make out two people. The taller figure looked like they were hovering over the shorter and I could hear a ripping noise. I rushed forward and immediately grabbed whoever it was into a body lock. When I looked forward, I saw red hair and I lost it. It was Isla. Blood was trickling down the side of her face and she was covered in tears. I felt a red haze come over me, and all I could feel was anger. I beat up the bastard over and over again, without a care in the world. I would've killed him if it wasn't for Isla crying out in pain.

I don't think she realized it was me until I called out her name. She looks up at me, and in that moment, I want to kill the guy, but right now, she needs me.

"Isla, did he break anything?" My hand is hovering because I'm not sure if she'll let me touch her after this. She looks down to assess her injuries, then reaches up towards her face, wincing when she touches her bloodied cheek. She shakes her head and begins to cry uncontrollably.

"Can I touch you? I want to make sure he didn't break anything and to help you cover up. I have to take you to the hospital." She cries even harder and shakes her head from side to side. I can't *not* take her the hospital; they need to be able to look her over.

Her body is shaking badly. I take a chance she'll be comfortable with me. I gently lift her head and try to look closely at the damage. She's got some scrapes along her cheek, as if he'd dragged her along the wall. I move slowly to see if I can help button up her blouse. He popped a few off, but it looks like I can cover most of her up.

"Isla, can you walk?"

She doesn't bother to look up at me. We shouldn't stay here much longer, so I place my hand underneath her, supporting her back. Using my legs, I lift her up and decide to walk her back to her dormitory. Maybe Charlotte can convince her to let me take her to the hospital. I glance over and see the fucker hasn't move. I don't bother stepping around him. Instead, I bear all my weight over his hand and step on it. I hear the crunch and he screams from his unconscious state. I adjust Isla in my arms and swing my leg back and pop him right in the face. His screams go silent and I leave him there; to rot, for all I care. Isla seems so small like this, and she curls in tighter against my chest, silently crying.

The walk is long and arduous, but I get her back to campus without incident. As we near her dorms, I feel her stir.

"I don't want to go back there," she rasps out.

"Isla, you need someone to watch over you. You might have a concussion or something worse, and you're refusing to let me take you to the hospital," I spit out. I don't want to leave her, but I don't think she'll be comfortable coming home with me after what happened.

"Please, Ben... Charlotte—" She can't finish her sentence. Instead, she cries into my shirt, mumbling something.

"Shhhhh, okay. I'll take you back to my room. Okay?" She nods her head and quiets down a bit. It's the weekend, so most of the guys are probably out partying, which means the dormitory is quiet. I make my way across the lawn, and easily able to get her into the building. I gently put Isla down as I get to my room. I have one arm propping her up, so I can keep her steady but still able to unlock the door. I turn on the lights and help her inside.

"Here, come sit down on my bed. I'll find you something to change into if you want." She nods her head while slowly making her way to my bed. She gently sits down and winces. I don't know if he kicked her or something worse, but she's having a hard time sitting up. I move to my drawer where I keep my t-shirts and pajama bottoms. I look through for my smallest pair, in hopes she won't swim in the clothes. I grab a new bar of soap from my stash of bathroom supplies, and a clean towel.

"Isla… Isla, open your eyes, baby." I gently coax her eyes open. She lifts her head and her lower lip wobbles. "I need you to stay awake for me awhile, okay? I just want to make sure you didn't hit your head." She nods.

"Here's some clean clothes if you want to change, and if you want to clean up, you can. The bathroom is right over there. My shampoo isn't that girly shit, but it'll do." She sits and stares at the stuff I left for her on the bed. "I'm going to step out to make a call."

"No!" She grasps my hand.

"Shhh… It's just to call Finn, to let him know you're here with me. He'll head over to your room since Charlotte will be there. Okay?" A lone tear drips down her cheek, and I'm unable to keep away any longer. I lean in and kiss her gently, and she relents, letting go of my hand.

I glance back before closing the door behind me. She looks completely defeated, so I quickly dial Finn's number.

My phone rings several times, and I hope maybe I can just leave him a message instead of telling him straight out what's going on.

"Aye, talk to me." Finn sounds cheerful and I pause, quickly trying to decide what to tell him.

"Hey, do you mind staying at Charlotte's? Just for tonight."

"Sure, mate, what's going on?"

"Ummm… Isla is over, and—"

"Ye dirty bird." He laughs. "I knew it! Finally, now Charlotte and I dinnae have to hear ye pining for that wee bonnie lass."

"No, it's not like that, something happened. I don't want to go into details." I hear him suck in some air and hiss.

"Is she okay?" His voice goes hoarse and he sounds agitated.

"I don't know, she… She doesn't want to go the hospital and doesn't want to see Charlotte while she looks like this."

Finn is a decent guy and I hope he'll understand what I'm asking of him. He and Charlotte are dating, and it's a lot to keep this kind of secret, but I figure one night won't do any harm.

"I can't lie—"

"Look, I'm not asking you to lie. Just give her the night to calm down, she'll tell Charlotte afterwards. She can't hide it." I grind my teeth, knowing that's the truth. From looking at her face, she'll bruise. She has very pale skin to begin with, so the bruising will be prominent.

"What happened to the bastard? Charlotte told me earlier she was going out with Peter Umbridge."

"I don't know, I left him in a heap. Broke a few bones," I spit out. There is a pause on the line, so long I think for sure Finn has hung up the phone on me.

"I'll call my brother tonight. Isla needs to file a report, but I think she can file it tomorrow after she's calmed down. If he says she should do it tonight, I'll call ye back."

"Your brother…"

"Aye, my eldest brother is a policeman here in the city. Take care of her and we'll see ye in morning. Okay?"

"Okay, man, see you in the morning." I close my phone and walk inside. Isla is still on the bed, looking down at her torn blouse, with tears silently dripping down her face.

"Hey, hey, it's okay. I got you." I sit with her on the bed, and she leans down, pressing her unhurt cheek to my shoulder. I wrap my arm around her body.

"My arm hurts, and I cannae get the blouse off," she whispers.

"Okay, do you want me to help you?"

She nods her head and cries some more. I look at her and wonder how I do this and keep her modest, because I'm sure she doesn't want me to see her like this. She looks up with her tear-stained face, her beautiful blue eyes puffy and red-rimmed from all the tears.

"Can you stand for me? I'll unbutton things, but do you think you can do the rest?"

She nods. "I won't be able to reach my bra." Her lower lip trembles again.

"That's okay. You can turn around, and I can unsnap it for you underneath your blouse. I'll be seeing very little of you, okay? I promise it'll be quick."

She nods and blinks several times. I quickly grab the things off my bed and head into the bathroom, where I turn the water on and wait until it warms up. When it feels just about right, I come back and see Isla staring into the bathroom. I walk over slowly and before I can reach for her blouse, she leans her head against my chest. I instinctually wrap my arms around her until her shaking stops. She tries to smile up at me, but it's not quite right.

"Okay, I'm going to unbutton now."

I reach out, silently thanking God she didn't flinch when I touched what remains of the buttons. It's hard not to see any of her porcelain skin, where she has freckles spread out along her chest. I see bruising forming lower down and I know immediately he'd grabbed her *there*. I try to control my anger because I don't want to scare her. I glance down and see her eyes are closed, which makes me more upset. As soon as the last button is finished, I move to stand behind her. I reach under her shirt and unsnap her bra. She moves her hand in front of her chest to hold the bra up.

With her head tucked down, I hear a small, "Thank you," coming from her and she walks quietly into the bath-room to rinse up. She's in the bathroom for longer than I like and I'm worried she'd hurt herself. I move to the door and put my ear to it, to see if I can hear anything. I can only hear water running, so I knock.

"Isla, is everything okay? Do you need any help?" I gently ask. I don't want to push my luck; me helping her undress was probably hard enough. The water shuts off finally and I hear shuffling around.

"Ummm… yeah, I used all your hot water," I hear her small voice say.

"That's okay. I just wanted to make sure you're okay. Take your time." I go back to my desk and shuffle about. I've got so much nervous energy, I don't know what to do with myself. All I wanted to do is protect Isla, and part of me feels like I failed her in so many ways tonight. I know she's not mine, but she felt like it. The door opens, and Isla steps out in only my shirt.

"Did the pajamas not fit?" I blink a few times, because Isla in just my shirt and no pants is a heady thing. I shouldn't want her like this, not after what happened, but she is beautiful.

"No, they kept falling down."

I move quickly to my drawers and pull out a pair of boxers. She might be able to roll these up enough to fit.

"Do you want to try these?" I hold up a pair of my navy-blue ones and she nods her head. The shirt she's wearing is enormous on her, almost to the point of it being a dress. I bring the boxers over and hand them to her. She picks up her feet to place her leg through the first leg, but has a hard time steadying. I step forward. "Here, I'll hold you steady," I rasp out.

My eyes are forward and I refuse to look down as she attempts to put the boxers on, which she's easily able to do now that I'm holding her up. She attempts to roll them over and I smile down at her as she gazes up at me.

"Let me do that." I smile and quickly roll them up as far as they go, then step back a little and see they'll hold up on her now.

"Thanks." She smiles at me, and this time, it doesn't seem as strained. She seems a little more relaxed now that she was to clean herself up. The bleeding from the scrapes have stopped, and while the bruise is prominent, I'm glad her eyes aren't swollen from the hit she took, except from the crying.

"Can I lay down now?"

I nod and lead her over to the bed, folding down the blanket so she can slip in. She easily climbs up and tucks into bed. I smile down at her and pull the blanket up to keep her warm, then kick off my shoes and walk over to my drawer to get a clean shirt. I turn around and whip off the one I was wearing, replacing it with a new one.

"I'll be right back, just gonna brush my teeth and stuff. I'll keep the door ajar, so if you need anything, I can hear you. Okay?"

"Okay." She smiles again, and tucks her head more comfortably against the pillow. I quickly get ready and slip on the pajamas pants she couldn't wear—might as well not waste a perfectly clean pair, since they're here already. I finish up and turn off the lights. Isla has her eyes closed and her breathing has become shallower. *Thank God I think she's fallen asleep.*

I jump into Finn's bed. He won't care, since there is no way I'm cuddling with Isla until she wants me to. Just as I'm about to fall asleep, I feel the bed dip and I immediately open my eyes.

"Isla?" I turn and see her trying to climb into bed with me. "Isla, what are you doing?" There is a little bit of light, not much, but enough to see her flinch a little. "Hey, no wait."

I reach out and caress her hand that's on the bed.

"I don't want to close my eyes alone," she whispers softly. "I just wanted…"

"Do you want me to hold you?" I almost missed it, but she nods slightly. "Baby, I need to hear you tell me." I gently coax her to say it aloud. I refuse to let her regret this, and I don't want any room of misinterpretation.

"Do ye mind?"

"No, I don't mind. I was trying to give you space."

"I feel safe with ye," she innocently tells me. I throw the covers off and hold my hand out. She tilts her head and looks at me questioningly.

I laugh. "Let's do this in my bed. It's a lot more comfortable."

She smiles and nods. We walk together to my bed, and I rock back into the bed first.

"I'll be big spoon if that works for you?" I cock my brow a little, hoping a little humor makes her feel more comfortable.

"Big spoon?"

"Yeah, you up front being little spoon, and me in the back. I think you'll be more comfortable like that. You can cuddle into me, and I'll keep you safe." I pat the bed and she snuggles right in. Before wrapping my arms around her, she shifts, getting into a comfortable position. She turns and surprises me with a light kiss on the lips.

"Goodnight."

"Goodnight, Ben. Thank you for saving me," she says tenderly.

"Always."

CHAPTER *twelve*

ISLA

IT'S BEEN A MONTH SINCE the day Ben rescued me from Peter. The first couple of days after the attack were rough for the both of us. I found out the next day Ben had told Finn, who then told his brother about the attack. Finn, Charlotte, and Finn's brother, Lewis, stopped by the next morning, to my surprise. Lewis was very kind and took some pictures of my injuries, so I didn't have to pop into the police station. He told me they'd found Peter checked into the hospital, refusing to say what had happened. He told them he'd been attacked, but the hospital had been suspicious about his story.

Charlotte was beside herself. She sat and held my hand throughout the interview, while Finn took Ben outside to cool off, and Lewis also wanted to make sure our stories were the same without hearing each other. At the time, I just wanted to forget the incident happened. I didn't even want to think about it because every time I did, it would make me sick. Ben insisted I tackle what happened to me head-on, and I am glad.

The attack put me in a bit of tailspin emotionally. I went from fear and confusion to embarrassment. Then, later, after some time to really take in what happened, anger. Ben felt guilty about letting me walk out the bar with Peter, and I felt stupid for getting that drunk. I blamed myself. We spent most of our time together, and Ben made a point to walk me home anytime I had to be out at night. It was a lot of nights in, sitting and watching the telly, eating in or even just sitting in silence, studying. All of it was comforting. It gave us time to just be together.

I kept apologizing for everything, I put Ben through the wringer, but he'd been patient with me. Peter got what he deserved. The university was swift after they received the police report from the attack, and he was rightly kicked out of school.

His parents tried to avoid jailtime, but bruises don't lie. Alcohol was no excuse, and later, I found out the boy I knew growing up wasn't the person I thought he was. *Nice* Peter had a temper on him and he'd gotten in trouble before. His father had his records expunged and money exchanges happened to make sure he could get into university without any complications. Lewis dug around and found out that little tidbit, and made sure everything was well-documented.

I spent a lot of time with Ben afterwards. I still don't even know if what we're doing constitutes dating, since we never "defined" that we were boyfriend and girlfriend. We still fight like an old married couple, but when you spend that much time with each other, it's much easier to get to know one another. Being around him feels uplifting and freeing. It's just *easy*. There's no pretense, and he likes me for me. I think he purposefully still picks on me, just to get me to fight with him. That he relishes in it.

Case in point, I'm here at the gym he frequents because I lost a bet with him about our second-to-last big test in class. He swore up and down he'd get a better letter than me, with less studying time. I took that bet because I thought he was being an eejit. I saw him crack open the book once before the test. When the professor handed our tests back, he'd beaten me by two points. Two stinking points.

"So, is this what ye young kids do for dates?" The owner of the gym introduced himself as Ferguson when Ben and I walked in.

"Ummm… I wouldnae call it a date. He's never asked me out before."

I smile at him as I watch Ben punch a really large hanging bag. Ferguson frowns at Ben after hearing me say that.

"Eh, you've got to ask a lass out if ye want to actually call her yer girlfriend. Haven't I taught ye anything?" He smiles back at me.

"Girlfriend? Can't call me his girlfriend either, if he doesnae ask." I smirk and watch as Ben turns towards us. His brows pull forward and he takes long strides towards me. He passes, and ignores, Ferguson, who looks like he wants to say something.

He wraps me up in his arms and leans in. "What do you mean, you're not my girlfriend?"

"Yeah, when have ye ever asked me out on a date?" I cock my brow and fold my arms across my chest.

"Last night, when I took you out for pizza…" He kisses me gently on the cheek. "The night before last, I took you out for ice cream." He kisses me lightly on the forehead. "I even gave you a piggyback ride back to campus."

He leans me back, and before I squeal, he covers my mouth and kisses me hard, like he owned it. His kisses were relentless, owning even, and I never wanted him to stop. He shifts me back upright and leaves me to myself and Ferguson.

He returns to his bags and begins to hit it hard. I watch as he punches faster and harder, his feet quickly moving around the bag. "Plus, you almost took out my back. If that isn't love, I don't know what is." He hits the bag harder.

"Did ye just imply that I'm fat?" My voice goes up a few octaves. Unbelievable. I made one comment about my feet being sore. *He* took it upon himself to pick me up and give me a ride.

"I did not. I think you're perfect just the way you are." He smiles and picks up his water bottle on the small table along the mirror.

If that isn't love. He hasn't said it aloud to me, but he just said it as if it were like breathing.

"Ahhhh, young love. It melts me heart to see yous together. Yer man over there is a good lad."

Ferguson is picking something out of his teeth and flicks whatever he dug out onto the floor. I nearly wanted to gag, he's pretty rank, but Ben loves coming here. If he's not studying or with me, he's here at the gym, working out and "getting life tips," is what he said to me once. But the way Ben talks about Ferguson, it sounds like he's been helping him out with something, but I didn't get a clear picture on what that was.

"Ummm..." He smiles kindly at me and his gaze has a slight twinkle, like he knows something but won't tell me. I smile back at him and glance over at Ben, who's moved onto another bag that is much smaller, but it's tied between two bouncy ropes.

"Does Ben come here to help every day?" I play stupid and see if he'll tell me Ben's secret.

"Oh, he works out here every day, but 'bout once a week, he helps with the books. The numbers scramble on paper for me sometimes. Makes it hard to keep the books straight. Ben here is a genius with numbers."

"He does your accounting?" I cock a brow.

"Aye, when I first met Ben, I happened to mention me wifey had been out of town helping our daughter out. I was left to my own devices with the books. It takes me all day to figure out what to do, and even then, I was getting it wrong. Ben is helping me with a system to help with my numbers. It's getting easier." He eyes Ben speed punching that funny little bag.

"Ben, shift a little more to yer right when you hook it like that." He goes about chewing on his toothpick. "I'll leave you kids alone; I'll be in the back if you need anything."

I watch Ben carefully on how quickly he's able to dodge that ball. Spending enough time with Ben, there is something special about him. I know it sounds cliché, but Ben is honest to a fault and incredibly helpful where help is needed. His goodness is inherent and pure. Even if we haven't said the words directly, I love him too.

CHAPTER

thirteen

T HE WEATHER IS GETTING COOLER. While the rest of the student body is still in classes, all of the program students were given the last half of the week off to prepare for our large business projects. Isla and I have been working harder to. We knew the "break" was coming up, so we decided be diligent with our time. Isla kept insisting we finish ahead of time, but she didn't explain why. I thought it was her Type-A, OCD, *I must have it all done* personality at play.

"So, I heard from Charlotte yer finished your big proposal?" Finn is finishing up one of his papers that's due today. I really don't know how he doesn't shit bricks, waiting so close to the end like this.

"Yeah, thank God. Because if I had to hear her telling me every single day that it needed to get done, I don't know what I would've done. I love her, but she's relentless." I laugh and grab a snack off my desk. My phone rings and I scramble to pick up since I know it's Isla. I set a specific ringer.

"Hey, babe." I rip open the wrapper and bite into the Lion bar. I know eating a candy bar isn't optimum, but I still need to pop into one of the shops to get some actual food.

"*Madainn mhath mo ghràdh.*"

"Did you just sneeze?" She snorts-laughs over the phone. She does this sometimes, in conversation, where she'll break out into Scottish Gaelic. Every once in a while, she'll tell me what she's saying.

"No, ye eejit… I said, good morning, my love."

"Ahhhh, I thought *gaol* meant love?"

"It does, but I used *mo ghràdh* instead."

None of this makes sense, and to be honest, I should be more sensitive. I'd asked Isla if it would be easier to learn to speak Gaelic, and she had the audacity to laugh. Once she calmed a bit, she told me it wasn't common tongue, but that she'd teach me a few words here and there. I responded by telling her I wanted her tongue all over my body, which caused her to blush.

"Where are you? I can meet up with you if you're not busy. Also, I'm hungry, so maybe we can pop down to Grassmarket where that breakfast place is." I shove the rest of the candy bar in my mouth. "Because I'm seriously resorting to candy," I mumble.

She laughs again, and it sounds like she's outside walking.

"Pack a weekend bag and meet me outside."

"Huh?"

"I said, pack yer bag and meet me outside." She enunciates every single word, like I didn't hear her.

"I heard you, Wildfire, I'm confused. Did we have plans and I wasn't paying attention? Where are we going?"

She's mumbling to herself and I can't really hear her, but it makes me smile. I get up and head to the closet to grab my duffle bag. I start shoving enough boxers and undershirts for the weekend. I don't bother with pajama bottoms, as Isla is used to me walking around with as little clothes as possible. I throw in a couple of jeans and shirts, but not knowing where we are going is making this difficult. I noticed Scotland is temperamental when it comes to weather and temperature. A couple of weeks back, we were caught up in snow. I couldn't believe it, but Isla acted like it was normal. *That* isn't normal.

Pulling the phone closer, I said, "No joke, where are we going, I want to make sure I pack the right clothes." She's still mumbling, something about me being a boy. "And sweetheart, I'm all man. Not a boy."

"Pack some warm clothes, and yer hiking shoes that I saw in yer closet. It can get a bit nippy where I'm taking ye." She's still not giving me any clues, so I throw in my warm coat and hoodie.

"Okay, babe, I'm gonna hang up. I'll be down in a minute. I love you."

"Love ye too."

I quickly grab my toiletry bag and throw it in, along with the book I'm reading. I tap on Finn's shoulder, since he's got a pair of headphones in. "Hey, Finn, you'll have the room to yourself. Isla is sneaking me off somewhere."

He smiles and puts his thumbs up like he understands, then continues with his paper. I look inside the bag and make sure I have everything. Grabbing my keys, phone, and charger, I head downstairs. I'm expecting to see Isla standing there, but when I get outside, she's not anywhere to be found.

Sitting outside is a lone car. The engine is still running since I can see the exhaust puffing out the back. It's a fancy, sleek, black BMW that looks practically new. I shift my duffle bag and decide to go around the side. Sometimes she waits there since she can see the view of the trees from there. Normally, I'm the one running a little late, so this is unusual for her. When she called, she made it sound like she was outside waiting for me.

The car honks at me as I begin walking, I turn and see the window is rolled down. "Hey handsome, fancy meeting ye here."

I step up and lean on the ajar window to see Isla with her hair pulled back and no makeup on.

"Hey, you little minx. Did you steal this car?" I cock my brow as she throws her head back and laughs.

"No silly, my mum let me borrow it for the weekend after I told her I wanted to show my friend Scotland." She smiles wide and reaches over to open the door, but I beat her to it. I know it sounds chauvinistic of me to think this, but I wasn't going to let her open the door for me. It's one of the few things I'm insistent on.

"Now that you have me, what shall we do?" I lean across the seat and kiss her hard. She always has kissable lips but today, right now, I just wanted to devour her. We haven't moved past second base. After that bastard attacked Isla, I wanted her to be one hundred percent comfortable with me. We've talked about doing more, but I've left it up to her to decide. I'm on *her* time, and I'm okay with that.

"I want to take ye up to Glencoe, where my nan's house is." I look at her big bright smile.

"Really?"

She nods her head. "It's close to three hours. We can stop along and grab some breakfast before heading out. But since it's early, I'd like to take ye to see Linlithgow Palace first. It sits upon a beautiful piece of land. Mary Queen of Scots was born there. You'll see her statue and everything.

We can stop in and have some lunch in Stirling and see the castle. It's similar to Edinburgh Castle, as it sits upon a big hill and you can see the city below. It's absolutely stunning."

"Isla, I would love to see your country through your eyes. I love it here, you know it."

She nods her head slowly and gives me a look. I'm not lying, I do want to see everything through her eyes. I don't tell her I've seen some of her country already, when I arrived, because what happens now is really all that matters. We've talked about the future together. We still have our senior year to finish up our studies, but we are both free to do what we want. Isla knows my plans to work with Cardona Financial, which got her excited. While her father would like her to go into the family business, she was told the world was open to her. I would marry her today, right now, if it weren't prudent. But the thought has been dropped—I can see myself living here permanently some-day, so long as she's with me.

Isla drives like a bat out of hell, and as we get out of Edinburgh, the roads get narrower and the number of cars drops off significantly. I had to close my eyes at some points because I really don't know how anyone drives around here. It's only wide enough for one car but Isla swears by the pull-offs. We decide to get to Stirling for breakfast since she said there was a lot to see there. As we get closer, we immedi-ately get hit by the view of the castle sitting up on a huge hill.

"It looks like the faeries cut the top off that mountain and man stuck that big castle up there." Isla slows down, glancing at me as I stare out the window.

"That's amazing. I can't even imagine having to walk up there way back then."

"Aye, there are well-documented stories about Stirling

castle. It's one of the strongest defensive castles, if not, the most. Bonnie Prince Charlie couldn't even take it."

She looks around and pulls into a parking space down below. We pop into one of the restaurants she said her father used to take her to, and I know they make a fantastic full Scottish breakfast. We spend the rest of the morning chatting and eating, and by the time we finish, I'm excited to walk the grounds of Stirling Castle. Isla doesn't think it's a good idea to take the car up as parking is difficult, so we buy bus tickets.

The tour is absolutely amazing. She slowly pulls me into each room, pointing to the paintings and architecture. It's amazing to watch her talk about Scotland's history. From first glance, it would look like she wanted nothing to do with history, but she has a deep love for her country.

It now makes sense why, of all the schools she could've attended, she chose to stay in Edinburgh. The day is long but I don't care, I cherish every minute I get to spend time with her because school is about to end.

We both decide to stop in and see Doune Castle since Isla knows how much I love Monty Python. I hadn't realized this is where they'd filmed that movie. When I see it standing there, all alone, after driving down a long narrow road, I'm in awe. We don't get a chance to go inside since it's closed off to the public, but I'm able to take a few pictures and walk the grounds. A little further off the side, there's a wooded area with a running stream. The place is eerily quiet, which is made worse because a roll of dark clouds starts to litter the sky.

We head back to the car so we don't get into Glencoe too late. I must have fallen asleep between Doune Castle and Glencoe, because I feel the car bounce a little and I pop open my eyes immediately. I look around and see Isla chuckling to herself.

"Hello, sleepyhead, we're here."

I rub my eyes and sit up to see a field of green and in front of us are high mountains. The tips of them can't even be seen because there seems to be a permanent fog hugging the tops. I lean forward, and from what I can see, below the mountains, is a cute white house with a dark gray roof.

"Oh wow!" I sit up some more and stretch as far as I can. Turning, I smile at Isla. Her eyes are alight but she seems to be nervous about something.

"You okay?" I asked, concerned something is wrong. I look around to make sure nothing is amiss.

"Everything is okay." She smiles widely at me. "I get like this when I come here. It's just, I dinnae ken how to describe it, but as soon as set my feet upon the land and smell the clean air, it feels like home even though I didnae grow up here." Her hands tighten and then loosen around the steering wheel. "I wish ye were here when the heather and thistles are out. It's just rows upon rows of purple and green."

"All of the land?" I point out in front of us as she slows down the car.

"Mmmhmmm, the whole field." She parks the car, and we both get out to stretch. I watch Isla as she slowly walks towards the house, as if she's forgotten I'm here. She pulls out a key from her pocket, but just as she turns it, she stops and turns around. There's something different in the way she is looking at me, but it seems to pass and she shakes her head.

Isla pops the trunk and walks back towards the car. I shake my head and she stops, curious.

"I'll get the bags, why don't you go in and get settled. You've driven the whole way." She tries to ignore me and continues walking forward. I quickly move around the car and grab her hand, pulling her back towards the house.

"Ben… I want to help." I shake my head again and kiss her at the doorway. Pushing the door all the way open, I place my hand on her back and gently push her forward.

"If you don't listen, I'll carry you in."

I kiss her again for good measure and run back towards the car to grab our bags. I see Isla packed several bags and I can't figure out why she's brought so many clothes. It's incredibly heavy, so I unzip it to see what it could be. It's a huge cooler full of food. I hadn't even thought about food. Being so secluded here, I can imagine there not being a lot of shops or grocery stores for us to grab anything. I guess we'll be cooking while here.

I finally get all the bags into the doorway, and when I step inside the chilly house, I hear a fire crackling in the background. I look around and it doesn't take me long to find Isla, who is leaning down near a fireplace, starting a fire. A small billow of smoke is going up the chimney and I see a small amber glow emanating.

"So, no heater?"

She turns and shakes her head. "It won't take long to heat up the house, plus, I packed some hot water bottles. We left all of my nan's blankets here too, for when we visit. We'll have to start the fire upstairs too." I nod and see there is at least a refrigerator in the corner, with a stove next to it. We both get to work, unpacking the huge bag of food.

By the time we're both settled in and get everything put away, we're pretty tired. Isla and I lounge on the couch and sit in comfortable silence, reading our novels. Isla is leaning on me, and she has her nose in what looks to be a romance novel.

"So, what's your story about? I'm reading about death and destruction." She turns her head slightly and looks up at me for a second, but doesn't answer me. "Isla—"

She moves her hand quickly, reaching up and placing it

over my mouth. I see the serious look on her face, so I await a response on what she's doing.

"Shhhhh… I'm not done yet." She releases me and goes back to reading. I can't believe she just shushed me. My girlfriend just *shushed* me over a book about sex. I place my book down and I reach over and snatch hers.

"Hey! Give me that back!" She turns and tries to reach out for it, but my arms are much longer than hers. She has no chance of getting the book back. I use my other hand to tickle her under her arms. "Stop! No… No, stop!"

She is laughing and kicking out, trying to get away from me. I throw the book across the room and she wears a look of horror as it flies and hits one of the sitting chairs. "You *arse*!"

She scrambles and tries to grab it, but I'm too quick for her. I'm able to grab her by the waist and place her back on the couch, where I pin her arms and smile down from my position on top of her. I place my knee on the ground so my whole body doesn't crush her. The half of me that is on her can feel her warmth and it's a heady sort of feeling. I lean in and kiss her, softly at first, but the second my lips are on hers, we both lose control. Isla throws one of her legs over my hip and tightens around me.

"Isla—" I moan and let go of her arms, and she immediately wraps them around my neck. I grind against her tight body and she cries out a moan. I can't do this with her downstairs, so I stop and scoop her up. Wrapping her other leg around me, she's now holding onto me like a spider monkey. She continues to kiss me like it's her last, and I open my eyes to see she's closed hers. I make my way with her up the stairs to the bedroom we set up together. I nudge the door open with my foot, glad to see the room has finally warmed up and it's glowing. I stop and pat Isla's bottom to get her to put her legs down.

Isla's eyes are heavy with need when I step back to take a breath, and I know I could get lost in her if I let myself. I need to know she wants this more than I do. I don't want her to have any regrets about us. I want her to *choose* me. She slowly steps back, then pulls off her shirt and unsnaps her bra. All I can do is stand there.

CHAPTER *fourteen*

Isla

For a second, I wondered if I made a mistake. That I misread what Ben wanted this whole time. He looked at me like I was the beginning to his end, and that feeling was mutual. I ached every time we were apart. I don't know what we're going to do. Our future was still not written, but I believe him when he says we'll work. This kind of love scares me, but it's worth the hurt and fear. Ben is worth it. He calls me his wildfire. I wasn't too keen on being thought of as an unrelenting burst of flames, but now I understand the analogy. He would *never* hurt me despite myself. He is so giving, to a fault, and he would *never* lock me into someone I'm not.

Despite us being so young, we made a promise to always find our way back to each other, even when things got difficult or we changed, because ultimately the changes would happen to both us. That love was enough.

I couldn't have him leave Scotland without having this

part of me. Wide-open and naked, both in the physical and the emotional sense. He knew my biggest fears and dreams, and he embraced them. I just wanted to rip all his clothes off downstairs when he grinded against me. I've wanted him for a long time, but I didn't know how to initiate it. It's one of the reasons I was pushing so hard to finish our assignment. It now gives us all weekend to get lost in each other.

When I looked at him, at first, he was shocked, and then awed, as I removed my clothes. I've never been more forward with a guy, but this is Ben. I wholeheartedly want this with him. To share myself in not only a place I love, but to have that love reciprocated. I have never felt a kind of love like this. It's about trust, and Ben wants nothing from me, other than me.

He helps me out of my clothes slowly, and I feel like I may burst into flames. I stand stock-still as I watch him strip out of his clothes, memorizing every muscle and dip in his body. The only way to describe him is just beautiful. He's semi-hard now, and I can't tear my eyes away as he walks up and caresses my body. I know I should be shy about being on full display, but being around Ben is easy. There is something about being in love and giving this part of yourself.

"I always wondered if you had freckles all over your body."

"I hate my freckles."

"I love your freckles; I want to kiss every single last one of them." He runs his hands lightly over my shoulders and kisses every part of me he touches, burning as he goes.

"Ben, I—"

"Shhhhh, I got you. Just relax." He continues to stroke my body, every touch warmer than the next. I feel like I could burst like the nickname he's given me, and lose control.

"Just let go, Isla, I'll catch you." He kisses and strokes me until I ache for him. My arms are locked in his embrace and I feel everything when he touches me like this. Protected and cherished. I never knew I could feel like this with anyone. My guard always up, but for him, I can let it down and not feel trapped.

"Please…" I feel his warmth leave me and I open my eyes to see Ben on his knees in front of me. He grabs hold of my behind and drags me forward, almost tripping me in the process. His warm laughter fills the air as he places a kiss along my hip bone, then licks downward to where I need him the most. I have nothing to grab onto except his golden-brown hair, as he licks and sucks.

"Isla, I could do this for the rest of my life and be the happiest man alive." I look down and see him gazing up at me. His eyes are intense, and I can see the truth swimming in them. This is our time. This is our forever.

He stands and picks me up, and I squeal in surprise as he carries me over to the bed, where I lay bare for him. My legs fall open, wide enough for him to take me. He's gentle at first, giving me time to adjust to his size, which isn't small by any stretch of the imagination. He is *perfect*. Leaning in a little further, he kisses me as he thrusts a little deeper, and I bite down a little harder than I mean to, which makes him moan.

He languidly moves in and out, as if savoring his time with me, before kissing me harder, demanding more from me as he moves a little faster. My hands caress down his tight back and I can feel the muscles bunch and release as he moves inside of me. Feeling his warmth is a heady sort of feeling and I would do this all the time if I could get away with it. Mixing the emotional with the physical is new for me. I've never loved anyone as much as I have Ben.

"Isla, get out of your head, baby. Wrap your legs around my hips." He motions and moves his hand up and down my legs, until I comply and tighten my grip around his hips so he can move faster. My body tightens as he hits a spot I've never felt before. I throw my head back as he kisses down my neck.

His thrusts grow more frantic and harder. I tighten my grip around his hips as he moves deeper, and that tingling feeling starts, the one I have no control over. He's playing with my body, building the tension and then slackening to prolong my orgasm. I just want to let go, but I can't until he lets me. My body begins to tremble.

"That's it," he whispers against my lips, and he thrusts two more times before I feel my body shake and I let go of the mouth that's all over mine, and come. When my body stirs and calms down, I open my eyes, and can't help but smile up at the face in front of me. Ben is looking at me adoringly, as if I were the moon to his star.

"I love you," I whisper.

"I love you, forever." He kisses me deeply, like it's the last kiss he'll ever get from me. We do this throughout the night, kissing and making love in the most magical of places.

CHAPTER *fifteen*

BEN

I WAKE UP TO WARMTH and softness, and snuggle in closer, feeling around until I have Isla totally in my arms. I tighten my hands around her without waking her, but she moans in her sleep. She's breathing heavily against my shoulder; her hair is askew and fanned out on my chest. I continue to caress every inch of her luscious body. I know it's wrong to worship anyone, but if this is wrong, I don't ever want to wake up. Isla has the kind of body you want to cherish. At first glance, you would think she was pixie thin, but underneath her clothes, Isla is all curves. And my God, the freckles. I was right, her body was fully painted with freckles. I know she hates them, but they make her more beautiful.

I was too rough with her last night, both of us getting lost in each other's bodies. I'd wondered if I would ever find this sort of bliss. I sure as shit didn't expect to find it here in

Scotland. I was just supposed to be here for my studies, but instead, I also found the other half of my heart.

We're locked, miles and miles away from school, with just each other. I think it's something we needed, even if last night never happened. The time we're getting now is so valuable, since we wasted so much of it misunderstanding each other.

"Hey." She softly kisses me, shifting to look in my eyes.

"Hey, my little Wildfire. I didn't mean to wake you up."

She shivers against my chest, so I try and pull up the blanket that has fallen off of her, but I can't quite reach it. The fire had finally died down by the time we passed out. I try to think fast on what to do, so I do the only thing I can —I rub her back to try and warm her up. She moans and shifts against me. If she's not careful, I'm going to get hard again.

"I want to go to New York," she whispers.

"Huh?" I look down at her and she kisses my chest, then looks up at me with her blue doe eyes.

"New York. I think after we graduate, I'll move to New York to be with ye." She says it with finality. I know we've talked about this, but we hadn't made a final decision. "I can go anywhere I want; Ah dinnae ken I'll have a problem getting a job over there. I dinnae want you to turn down that job. Mr. Cardona is personally training ye, that's not something ye get anywhere, Ben. Plus, ye said it yerself, ye couldn't wait to work with Toby."

I bite my lip and look at her adoringly. I don't keep secrets from her. When we were talking about how we would handle the future together, she knew Mr. Cardona was footing the bill and that his intentions were eventually to bring Toby and I along to run his company. She knows my financial situation and doesn't care. Spending all our time together, we've learned a lot. I learned she wasn't *too* proud, that I misconceived her as being a spoiled, rich kid.

Isla is anything but.

"I don't want you to give—"

"I wouldnae be giving anything up. I would be gaining *you*, and there is no price I wouldnae pay to have our forever be together." She climbs up my body and straddles my hips. We are both still naked, and having her body on top of mine is just too much to ignore. I reach out and run my hands down her chest, committing every curve of her hips and her breasts to memory. Even in the early morning dawn, I can see her carrying our child someday and us growing old together.

She leans forward, giving me the closeness I desire, and I kiss her long and hard. I pull her hair back and tuck it behind her ears so I can kiss her without any distractions, then make love to her again until the sun rises.

CHAPTER *Sixteen*

B EN AND I WERE LATE to leave Glencoe, neither one of us wanting to leave that house. Promises were made for a forever. Instead of coming back when we were supposed to, we chanced leaving a day later, since we knew our project was finalized before leaving Edinburgh. I think I nearly gave Ben a heart attack as I drove in the Highlands. The roads were narrow and wet most of the time, and logically, it should've only been able to hold cars going one way, but we manage to drive the roads as if it were meant for two lanes.

We made it just in time to quickly shower and grab our things. The presentation went really well, and we are still waiting for our final grades, which we're hoping to get back today during class. The final project was in front of a panel of professors, including the dean of the university, and each professor held a percentage of the final grade. Ben and I worked collaboratively to come up with a business model that would handle both local venture capitals and international ones, based off our working knowledge and studies. We both came to the table with a different perspective, and because both of us are competitive, we rowed a few times throughout the weeks leading up to the presentation. Finn and Charlotte had left us to our whims on several occasions.

Ben and I both hold hands as we make our way to the business hall.

"Do you think we'll get our grade back?" I look up at him while he continues moving us forward.

"I don't know, but why do they have to take so long to grade? It's not like they saw it again. I've never had to wait this long at Harvard." He takes a sip of his coffee but glances at me. "By the way, did I tell you how beautiful you look?"

"Yes, several times." I smile, because I know the pair of jeans I'm wearing are his favorite. They hug me in all the right places, giving me curves I don't really have. He lets go of my hand, but before I can scold him, he places his hand on my butt.

"Hey!" I swat at him and try to remove it because while I love his hands all over me, I don't want it on full display in front of class. He has the audacity to laugh and give my arse a good squeeze. I narrow my eyes and sneer at him, but he just smiles right back and throws his arm over my shoulder, then leans in and kisses my temple.

We change subjects and talk about what he's planning to do when he goes back to Harvard, and some of the classes he's planned to take. He briefly mentions moving here and transferring. I'm not sure if he's just joking or being serious, but I *refuse* to let him do that. I won't keep him away from graduating. We are still young, but I think we can make it work even though it'll be long distance. We both have a future and the world's the limit, seeing we both are going to graduate top of our class and from prestigious schools. Very little can deter that now, especially since we are almost done. We will both be in a position to be together somehow.

We both walk into class together, and as we make our way down, several sets of eyes look towards us. "Are people staring at us?" I ask, and he looks around. He nods, but just shrugs. We did let go of our hands, so it's not like we're showing any real PDA. I'm not sure what's going on.

Class begins and the professor is talking about international law and how it applies to the business. We both take excessive amounts of notes about the different cases where we've seen businesses swindle and hide behind international laws to rip people off.

"All right, class, I have to cut the teaching short today due to an appointment, so ye can thank me later." The professor just smiles and laughs to himself. "But before I leave, I would like to hand back yer grades for yer final projects. The other professors and I have spent a great deal of time reviewing yer written proposals and oral presentations. We tried to be as constructive as we could, but congratulations to ye all. You've far exceeded our expectations, and we all believe each and every one of ye will have bright futures. Class dismissed."

He places each proposal next to each other.

"I'll get it." Ben stops me from moving. As he leaves, one of the other students—I think her name is Megan— comes up to me before heading out. "Oh, Isla, I'm so sorry."

"Wait, what?" I turn and try to ask her what she's sorry about, but she walks off too quickly. I start to worry Ben and I failed our final project, but how would she know? I look around and a few people are staring at me, pointing. I look down and make sure nothing is out of the ordinary. Before I can ask someone what is going on, Ben comes strolling up the stairs. He's got a big smile on his face.

"Isla, look!" He waves the proposal in my face and I can't help but smile, forgetting all the weirdness happening around me. I grab our proposal and open it up.

On the front cover there are paragraphs of written notes from some of the professors. Words like *innovative* and *smart* stick out, but at the very bottom, there is an "A" and a note of congratulations that we won the final project. I squeal and throw my arms around Ben, and he hugs me back.

"I'm so proud of you," he whispers against my ear.

"Takes two, congratulations too!" He squeezes me tightly and kisses my cheek. When we pull back, most of the class has left, except for a few who still have their heads in their proposals. Ben grabs my hand and walks us out of the building.

"Let's go celebrate now!"

I shake my head at his enthusiasm. "We can't, we both have classes."

He grabs and swings me around and I throw my head back and laugh.

"I don't care, I feel like celebrating!" He slows down, thank God, or I was going to throw up.

"You know we can't." I kiss him before he puts me down on my feet.

He groans. "Okay, later then. We can call Charlotte and Finn, maybe go get drinks?"

"Sure, okay." He leans in and kisses me before we say goodbye. I watch as he walks in the other direction. We don't share the next class together, and I have a little bit of time before my next, so I decide to head back to the dormitory. When I get closer towards my room, I see my father standing out in the hallway. He's got his suit on and I can see his hair looks a bit tossed about. He must've heard me walking because he turns his head towards me.

I smile wide. "Da! What are ye doing here? Did the professors call ye about our project?"

He blinks several times, but instead of smiling, like I expected, his mouth thins. *Shite.* I quickly think why he might be upset at me. I know I told my mum about Ben, and I didn't intentionally keep him a secret, but maybe he's upset I haven't introduced Ben to them.

"Da—"

"Isla, can we talk inside?" He looks around the hall, like he's scanning for people.

"Uhhh, sure. Let me open the door." He scoots aside to give me room, then walks in behind me and closes the door. I turn to see grim lines marking his face, and he looks incredibly tired, like he's not slept for months.

"Da, what's going on?"

"So, ye havenae seen the news?"

"No, I've been busy…" I watch my Da walk over to my desk and pull out the chair. "I need ye to sit down, Isla."

"Okay." I blink a few times, then plop myself on the seat he's offered. He looks around and grabs Charlotte's chair, then sits across from me.

"We've hit a bit of a problem with the company." He holds no punches; he just spits out that information.

"Okay, what kind of problem."

"An illegal one, Isla…" He sighs and rubs his eyes, as if he were going to cry, but I've only seen my Da cry once, and that's when my nan died.

"What do ye mean?"

He doesn't answer me at first, and it feels like the bottom drops out. I know my Da, he's an honest businessman. What could he have done that would cause an illegal problem to arise?

"The police stopped by the office. They'd been investigating Andrew for months for illegal financial activities."

I swallow hard. "I'm confused. Why would they be investigating and not notify you? You've done nothing illegal," I spit out.

My Da has his head down and I pray he hasn't broken the laws.

"I haven't, Isla, but they didn't know that. They haven't finished yet, but the most damning of the investigation has come out. They arrested Andrew last night in his home." He sucks in a breath. "I was notified last night that the authorities would be in contact with me, and I was shown this morning what they've found. Andrew has been siphoning off funds from our clients for years. At first, it wasnae noticeable, but it became glaringly obvious recently."

My Da's hands begin to shake. I reach and grab his, squeezing them in mine.

"Da, what are ye going to do?"

"Ah dinnae ken, Isla… Ah dinnae ken. I've hired a lawyer. I must protect yer mother, brother, and you as much as possible. It doesnae look good, but I need ye to come home after term is over."

"Da—"

"I know you've made plans with that boy, but I cannae have ye away during this time. Yer mother will need ye. Yer family. Ah dinnae ken how long this will take. That clarty bastard swindled a lot of our clients."

My father leans forward and puts his hands on his head. I've never seen him this upset. Now I know why all the students were looking at me during class.

"Da, did the news break about Andrew being arrested?"

His eyes glance up to mine and he nods his head. I quickly cover my mouth.

"I'm hoping we can weather the storm, but ah dinnae ken. It's not good. The office has been getting calls nonstop from reporters, but a lot of our clients are demanding an audit of their accounts. Andrew had access to them all. We'll be ruined, the MacDonald named dragged through the mud. No one will want to work with us after this."

My Da breaks down and cries, which in turn, makes me cry. I don't know what to do except hold him tightly. My father is a proud man, and for him to have to come here and tell me what was going on had to be humiliating. When he finally leaves to go home to look after our mother, I leave Ben a message to call me back as soon as possible.

I don't even make it to class. I don't think I can show my face after hearing about what happened, and I have the early beginnings of a headache coming on. I shut off all the lights, then curl up in bed and try to close my eyes, but I'm left to cry by myself for what's about to happen. I must've dozed off because I'm awoken by a knock at the door. I glance over and see it's only been an hour since my Da left. I drag myself out of bed and crack open the door to see a concerned Ben standing there.

"Hey—" He pushes open the door and wraps me up in a big hug, and I cry against him. "Shhhhhhhh... It'll be okay. I'm here."

He closes the door and carries me to my bed, where he lays down with me. Out of all the things that could happen today, I never expected to both ace my project and be told that devasting news. Ben just holds me close and lets me cry it out. I don't have the heart to tell him it doesn't look like I'll be able to come to Pennsylvania for Christmas break.

We'd spent a great deal of time talking about our future. At the time, everything felt certain, but now that I just got this news, it didn't feel like that anymore. *The MacDonald name will be dragged through the mud*, keeps ringing in my head over and over. My Da wasn't just talking about the company, but all of us. I'm a MacDonald. A MacDonald who's majoring in Business. Who would want to hire me after finding my connection? My plans were to graduate and go to New York with Ben, where maybe that stink wouldn't follow me.

After a while, I sniffle and rub my nose on his shirt. "How'd ye find out?" I rasp out. My throat feels dry and scratchy after all the crying.

"I got a call from Toby. He said it hit over there. He and his dad were watching the news break over breakfast. He was a little concerned." He rubs my back to soothe me.

"All the way there," I whisper to myself.

"Yeah, but it'll be okay." He kisses me on top of my head.

"Ye said Toby's dad was worried?"

"Mmmhmm… Yeah, Toby said something to the effect of it being a big deal. He was a bit worried."

Fuck. What am I supposed to do now? Ben was slated to work for Cardona Financial after graduation. Every situation flashes before my eyes. What happens if they associate Ben with me, and he later has problems with their clients? I couldn't do that to Ben. I just couldn't. It would kill me to ruin his life because of my name. I begin to cry some more because now everything is muddled and confusing, leaving me with a heart-wrenching decision to make.

CHAPTER *seventeen*

BEN

ISLA IS REALLY DISTANT, AFTER her father showed up to see her. We only have a little bit of time before I have to fly back. I've tried everything to coax her out of her shell. She just seems sad, despondent even. Every time I ask her what's wrong, she just starts to cry, and keeps excusing it as being under stress. But I know it's something else, it feels like something else. She's distant during the day but then at night, she curls up tight against me, like she's afraid I'm going to be leaving her.

Right now, we're having breakfast in my room since she spent the night here. She didn't want to go out to eat so I brought breakfast to her. I try to coax her into eating some of my breakfast, since I know whatever rubbish she asked for, she isn't going to touch. She has a knack for eating my food instead of hers, saying mine tastes better. Every time, I point out she should've gotten what she wanted instead of what she *thought* she should eat.

"Hey, Wildfire, what's going on?" She continues to push around the porridge she requested. I really don't know how she eats that stuff; it looks like paper mâché. "Hey, talk to me."

I grab her hand to stop her movements, then tilt my head down to see her face, which is now covered by her hair. But I don't mistake the tears that are falling down her cheeks.

I get up and grab her, and she simply slumps over instead of yelping like normal. She wraps her legs around my hips when I carry her back into the room, and I can feel the warmth of her tears running onto my chest.

"Shhhhh… Hey, everything will be okay." I rub her back and sit down, her body against mine, straddling my hips.

"No… it won't," she mumbles into me.

"Isla, I can't understand you while you mumble into my chest. I know I feel good, but I want to understand you, baby." I try to lift her chin so I can see her face, but she tucks in tighter. I continue to hold her tight and try to soothe her crying, but nothing seems to be helping. Her body is tight and she's shaking now. I really want to understand what is going on. Finally, her cries slow and she tries to pull off of me, but I won't let her.

"Hey, hey… calm down… Are you ready to talk now?" She rubs her red-rimmed eyes and tries to wipe the little bit of snot running down her nose, but I help her out. Her eyes snap forward and she scrunches up her nose in disgust.

"Ben! That's disgusting." Tears start to fall as she tries to laugh-cry at whatever seems to bother her.

"It's okay, I'll always wipe your snot away. Isn't that love?" I smile down at her.

"I can't go to visit you for the holidays." Her chin wobbles, as if it pained her to say the words.

"Okaaaay… That's okay. We can work it out another time." She begins to shake her head back and forth, but no words come out. "I don't understand, Isla. What is going on? You're scaring me."

"I dinnae want to do this."

"Do what? This, as in, us, or something else?" She just sits in silence; I can feel her tremble, like she's cold, but she's not. "Talk to me."

"I cannae do this to ye."

"Do what?" I grab her shoulders and shake her a little because she refuses to look at me. Her eyes snap forward and more tears begin to form.

"Ye have a future, Ben."

"Okay, so do you. We talked about this. We can make this work. We can make us work. I know it'll be hard, but come on, Isla. We have all the time in the world. I love you. And you love me. I heard you say it to me in your nan's house. That's enough. You're enough. I would *never* cheat on you. *Never*. This"—I point to her and me—"we matter. I will wait for you."

More big, fat tears fall down her beautiful face. "I cannae, Ben. Ye have a future."

"What is going on, Isla? Why do you think you don't have a future? Are you sick?" Goose bumps trail up my arms and I have a sick feeling at the pit of my stomach. I know she's been down after the news breaking about her father's company. I know it's a big deal, but maybe the something I was feeling was this. I hope to God she's not sick, I don't think I could bear it.

"Please tell me you're not sick, please, Isla." I grab hold of her and hug her tight. Her tiny fists are grasped in front of my shirt as I hold on.

She shakes her head. "I'm not sick, Ben, but there is no future here for ye… Or me. I cannae have ye dragged into my *family's* mess." She pulls slightly back, and I see determination and honesty flash in her eyes.

"Isla… That can't touch me."

"Yes, it can!" She screams it out as if she had it all bottled up inside, and I wince. "Ben, my Da came down to explain to me what happened. It's not good. The MacDonald name will be dragged through the mud and I cannae drag ye along with it. Ye have a future, see. A future. One with so many dreams. Dreams I cannae be a part of. You'll be associated with me. No one will hire ye. Yer friends will want to steer clear of me. I'm tainted."

"Stop, Isla. You don't know what you're saying. You are not the embodiment of your family. You can't take that on yourself. You *will* have a future, and it's with me. I'll protect you. *Us*." I try to pull her in tighter, but she climbs off of me before I can get a good grasp. When Isla decides on an action, she follows through. She just needs to give me time to convince her otherwise.

"Ben, I won't ruin ye. You'll see, two, three, ten years from now. You'll be successful. You'll give yer family everything ye ever hoped for. It just won't be with me." Her shoulders shake as she cries some more. Her head drops to her chest and she hugs herself tightly. She turns, but before leaving, I hear her whisper, "I love ye. I always will."

She quickly rushes out of the room and slams the door behind her. My head isn't able to catch up to what just happened. My heart just walked out that door, and I don't know if I'll ever be able to get her back.

Isla

The wind is howling along the twisted hills. This little piece of heaven along Glencoe is special, as if the faeries had carved it out themselves. *A tale my nan once told me.* The dreamer in me still believed in the faeries and the magic they held. How could I not? This little part of Scotland is beautiful, breathtakingly so. And I'm about to lose what little happiness I hold here.

My wayward auburn hair is flying everywhere as the wind picks up. I didn't bother to tie it back when I woke up this morning. I was too excited to even bother getting dressed properly, something I know my nan would have scolded me for. *Children don't run amok along these hills, especially after a cold, morning storm.* But I couldn't help myself, I wanted to feel the wet grass upon my feet and just stand out here to watch the sunrise break through the dark, stormy clouds. *Just one last time.*

It's breathtaking to behold, the light just beginning to hit every nook and cranny on top of the hillside. The wind picks up as I eye the field of thistles and heather that grow on our lands. Every memory locked away for safe-keeping. It's something I have to do, or I don't think I could manage. I'm good at walking away now.

After I walked out of Ben's dormitory, he tried everything he could do to *fix* us, but what was there to fix? We weren't broken. I loved him then, and even still now. I just risk assessed I wasn't good news for him and walked away. I wouldn't be responsible for his ruin. So, I broke his heart. He continued to write me letters I refused to open, until eventually, the letters stopped, and when they did, I cried for weeks. *I've lost him forever.*

This right here is the last thing I have to let go of. I feel as if I'm on a precipice, and this is my last chance to look upon my nan's land. I begged my father to keep it, but we had no choice. *We must pay our debts.* It was the last thing that had to go, with the company in shambles, riddled in scandal. Sadly, not even due to anything but trusting the wrong people.

My Da's partner, Andrew Wilson, had been swindling his clients for years. He'd been cooking the books, making everything on the up and up when, in fact, he'd been pocketing the funds and hiding it in his own overseas bank accounts. For an investment firm, this was a big no-no. To steal in that world was a death sentence, which meant our name was dragged through the mud.

The almost two-year investigation showed my Da had no knowledge, since the firm was set up in a way where one hand, to some extent, didn't know what the other was doing. *Negligence* was at play but no criminal offense. We'd been lucky enough to walk away, but not unscathed. Restitution had to be paid to those affected. We were lucky the investigators were able to track most of the money stolen, but the fines were astronomical. Mr. Wilson was found guilty and is currently serving time in prison for all of his crimes.

The time it took to investigate gave my father enough time finish paying out my schooling, and my brother Ian was just about to start school at Oxford on a partial scholarship. As much as my mum and Da wanted him here in Scotland, they understood why he felt compelled to apply elsewhere. The "MacDonald stink," as my brother put so kindly one day, was a real thing.

Every job application I sent in was "kindly" declined. One company went so far as stating they would, "under no circumstance, hire me," being that I was the daughter of Craig MacDonald. That letter was a blow to not only me, but my parents, as that firm was my first choice. I graduated with honors from the University of Edinburgh with a double major in Finance and Strategic Economics, and a minor in Statistics. I was a numbers girl, and what happened to my Da wouldn't deter me to change my major, even with the scandal over my head. Even with all my hard work, I had a degree and recommendations from the top professors at Uni—things that would do me no good here. As much as it hurt, it killed my father to watch disappointment after disappointment show up in our mailbox.

Despite my father paying through the nose in barrister and investigator fees, we were in salvage mode. He wanted his children happy, healthy, and with proper employment, so I was forced to apply overseas, and he was forced to consolidate all our funds for a modest living.

I finally got a job as an executive assistant in London, in a conglomerate that dealt with security. It wasn't in finance, but I hope my hard work and tenacity would move me up in the company. That in a few years, all the stink of what happened here in Scotland would be long forgotten, and I could actually do what I wanted. To apply the years of knowledge built at university in a career.

Our home outside Edinburgh was sold a few weeks ago, and my nan's home and the land would be put up for sale in a few weeks. I made it a point to spend a little time here before moving to London, saying goodbye to everything I know and love. This little piece of heaven is locked away safely in my memories. The memories of my time here with Ben would be safe. My heart ached where it should be joyous. I learned to knit in this home, my first shot of whisky was had on these hills, and I learned both love and heartache here. *My first true kiss. My first everything.* I don't regret my time with Ben, and I learned not everything is permanent. For a girl in her early twenties, that is okay. I'm comfortable knowing what I had to give up. I couldn't keep Ben here forever. He and I had a future, I know that for sure. Just not with each other.

"Isla… Isla, didn't you hear me calling?"

"Miss MacDonald, are you even paying attention?"

I look up to see Mr. Flanagan waving his hands in front me. His portly face is dotted with red splotches, fingers tapping away at the desk, as if annoyed by my presence. I'd been daydreaming about Glencoe and Ben. I tried not doing that because the thoughts would just make me depressed. My nan's house was sold so many years ago when my Da was trying to clean up the mess Mr. Wilson had made. After that day, before I left to come here to work, I'd never gone back home. I hadn't had the heart to go back to the place I loved the most. It'd only be a reminder of what I lost.

"Oh, Mr. Flanagan, I'm so sorry. I was thinking about

something Mr. Hills mentioned during the meeting. I'd forgotten that ye needed the filing papers. I got them signed too, so ye wouldn't have to go to the trouble of going to the top floor." Thinking fast on my feet, I shuffle through the papers in front of me. *I know I have them here, somewhere.* My hands brush through the papers quickly as I scan each document. "Ahhh… here they are."

Grabbing them from the bottom of the stack, I pass them to Mr. Flanagan's awaiting hands.

"Quick thinking, Miss MacDonald. Next time, try not to daydream so much. Not very professional, if you ask me," he huffs out, as if he'd just run a long marathon. "Make sure that you get Arnie to sign off on the expenses too. You'll need to do that ahead of the trip."

My eyes snap up. "Mr. Flanagan—"

But he was already walking away, in the opposite direction.

Perplexed, I walk towards Mr. Hills' office to talk to Cary first, before I go to grab a snack. I'd been working as the second lead executive assistant under Mr. Hills for the last year, and he'd never mentioned having to travel, ever. Cary would know what's going on. I see Cary at her desk, and her face lights up when she sees me approaching. She's been vital in me moving up in the company. Quite frankly, I've learned more under her than I would any other firm executive. She's quick-witted, sharp, and knows our boss's accounts better than he does. I don't think this office would run as smoothly if she wasn't in charge.

"Well, look what the cat dragged in." She smiles up at me as she continues typing away at the computer. She's incredibly talented at multi-tasking.

"Morning, Cary. I was going to pop over next door to grab some biscuits and some tea for the afternoon. Would ye like anything?" I shuffle my feet a little, waiting for her reply. She bites her lower lip, and I recognize her hesitation. I know she's been trying to lose some weight. I keep telling her she's beautiful, and to stop worrying about the two stone she had gained while pregnant. I know for fact her husband looks at her adoringly, and doesn't mind the extra weight she'd put on. *For God's sake, she was growing a little human.*

"I really shouldn't, I still have a stone left to lose," she whispers, so the rest of the office doesn't hear.

"How about I just pop over for some tea if the biscuits are a problem?" I tap on her desk. I know she probably hadn't gotten up yet, except to stop at the loo.

"Very well, just some breakfast tea, a splash of milk. No sugar. Thank you, Isla, it's very sweet of you to ask." She smiles and is about to get on with the rest of her typing.

"It's no problem, Cary. I dinnae want to bother Mr. Hills, but do ye know anything about a trip I'm supposed to take?" I whisper. I really do feel like a silly cow for asking, because I'm afraid I missed something. My mind has been thinking of home the last few days, and that's a distraction I don't need.

Cary begins to giggle, like she's holding in a secret. Getting up from behind her desk, she crosses over to me and gently tugs at my arm to follow her into one of the empty conference rooms. She places her finger over her mouth. "Shhhh… I'm not supposed to say anything."

She looks around to make sure no one is around to eavesdrop into our conversation, then closes the door behind her.

"What's all the secrecy for?" My hands are sweaty. I don't like secrets and being kept in the dark. But I breathe a sigh of relief it's not something I missed in conversation, for that had to be far worse than just not being told.

"Mr. Watson asked for an executive assistant to accompany him on his trip downtown. There is a huge meeting being set up with an American finance firm and Dillinger. Obviously, Mr. Hills thought I'd be best, but I can't with Alexander. So, I recommended you." She smiles widely. "Mr. Hills was going to talk to you earlier about it, but he got shuffled off to the next meeting. So, just act surprised when he makes his rounds later."

"I don't understand, why all the secrecy?" Cary begins to giggle again; it's her mechanism for all things. Whether she's happy, sad, or angry, she will bust out into a fit of giggles.

"Because, silly, it would mean a promotion if he likes you. Rumor has it that his executive assistant is close to retiring. It would be a test of sorts, so don't muck it up and don't tell anyone I told you," she says cheerfully.

"But…"

"No buts on this, Isla. I wouldn't take the job, even if they offered it to me, so don't worry about me. Plus, Watson has been snooping around in your resume. He knows you were top of your class at Uni, and that you're just rotting away in this job. You're better than any executive assistant… besides myself, of course." She grabs my hands and gently shakes them. "I know what happened to yer father seems to trail ye like a big piece of horse dung. Ye wear it like it's some Scarlet letter, even though ye hide it well. So, don't play no lies with me. I've worked with ye for several years. Smart as a whip, quick on yer feet. Ye got a fire in ye, and I'm not just talking about yer beautiful red hair—"

She giggles even more. Cary grew up in Glasgow for a few years, even though she's lived here most of her life, and her Scottish brogue seems to always peek out when she's riled up. Tilting her head slightly, she nods. "But just know yer well-liked around here. It's about time ye see that for yerself. Stop hiding yerself. Now, go get it." She smiles and gives me a squeeze before walking out of the conference room.

"Don't forget, no sugar, please." She pops back out quietly, as if we weren't skulking about the hallways, which leaves me to stand in the dark room by myself, thoughts and feelings swirling about. This would be a good opportunity, and just maybe, I'd be able to utilize my studies. I'm grateful for the years spent here at the security firm, but I'm a numbers girl, through and through.

A promotion would give me an opportunity to make my parents proud, not that they aren't already, but every time I talk to my Da, he has a way about him—not exactly happy or sad, just sort of ghostlike. The scandal took its toll on him, left a sort of guilt I don't ever blame him for, but we don't talk about such things. At the end of the day, I know my Da is a good man. He did everything possible to protect us.

CARY WAS RIGHT. MR. HILLS CALLED ME TO THE OFFICE later that afternoon and asked if I would accompany Mr. Watson to the meeting downtown the next day. Since the firm was handling the security and logistics of the meeting with Dillinger and Cardona Financial, it would be required for us to be available whenever they needed.

When I heard Cardona Financial was involved, I prayed I wouldn't run into Ben. Like a creeper still in love, I saw he was working for the firm. His photo wasn't displayed on their website, but a small biography was on there. He was Vice President of Acquisitions. Since this deal with Dillinger seemed less an acquisition, I figured the chances of seeing him would be slim.

Mr. Watson's executive assistant was on another assignment, so he wouldn't be able to participate. I knew the ins and outs, but was given a crash course on what was needed of me that went beyond executive assistant level. I'd met Mr. Watson once in passing, as he handles the more senior security accounts.

The next day, we checked into the Four Seasons near Hyde Park, all expenses paid by the company. I met him in the lobby later where he seemed more stiff than usual, cold even. I wasn't put off by it, as Mr. Watson seemed keen on my financial studies and incorporating them into whatever Dillinger needed.

"Isla, I will need you to head up to the executive level suites for the boardroom setup. Some of Cardona Financial executives are up there. I need you to make thorough notes as I talk to the hotel's security." I nod and quickly head towards the elevators. The Four Seasons lobby area is immensely beautiful. London has a different feel than Edinburgh. I haven't been home in a long time, and I missed it a lot. I lost my heart there, in more ways than one.

I ride the elevator all the way to the top executive suites, and when I come off, I hear deep voices mumbling. I make my way around the corner where I know the main area is, and see two men with their backs turned to me. One of them, from what I can tell, is an older gentleman with salt and pepper-colored hair. He's wearing a gray suit while the other man on his left is wearing a deep navy suit. From the look of the cut, both suits are very expensive.

Something about the man on the left seems familiar, but it couldn't be Ben. This man here looks taller and Ben had curlier hair. Plus, Ben hated suits, but I have an odd feeling sink into the bottom of my stomach. I shake it off as being nervous about the trip—if I do well, there's a good opportunity I could be promoted.

Not to scare them, I cough to get their attention. They

continue to talk, finishing whatever conversation they were having. The older gentleman turns around first, and I immediately recognize him as Sebastián Cardona.

"Hello, sorry about being rude. We just needed to finalize some things. You are?"

"It's no worry, Mr. Cardona. I will be assisting Mr. Watson. He asked that if ye needed anything, please don't hesitate to ask."

"I didn't catch your name, darling." He smiles politely at me.

"Oh, I'm sorry, it's—"

The man in the blue suit turns around, and I drop the briefcase I'd been carrying.

"Isla MacDonald. I would recognize that Scottish brogue from a mile away. It's nice to see you again."

THE END

Summer Love (A Forever Series Novella) –

mybook.to/SummerLove

Forever Love (Forever Series Book One)

mybook.to/ForeverLove1

Follow-up to Chasing Wildfire is Catching Wildfire

acknowledgments

First, I want to thank the readers for taking the time to reading Ben and Isla's story. And yes, I ended it on a cliffy. So, a little… okay big explanation of why.

When I finished up Forever Love, I expected to follow it up with Jamie's story but Ben's voice kept getting louder and louder. I knew he had a back story with Isla, but I wasn't sure what it was until he started shouting in my head. I made the tough decision to put Jamie's story off to write Ben's and couldn't believe what was unfolding.

Scotland.

I never had the intention of writing a story in Scotland. I didn't think I could do it justice for one, since I can never truly put into words what it's like visiting there. Like Ben mentioned, Scotland is magical in every sense of the word. I could've picked up Ben and Isla's story where it was in Forever Love, but as I began writing Chasing Wildfire, I realized it would require way too many flashbacks. For me personally, as a reader, too many flashbacks can be bothersome. you lose the emotions and the why. Ben and Isla's story is not complicated, but I thought it would've done you, the reader, a disservice if I didn't talk about where their story began.

Boy likes girl. Girl kind of hates boy. But ultimately, they fall in love. So that is where the second chance happens. Long story short, that is why their story is a duet.

I'm currently writing Catching Wildfire, which will be a fast forward to them where Forever Love left off. Isla is sassy as ever and well Ben will be the Ben you know and love, but the passing of time does change him a bit. He's still smarter than Toby, and he's determined is all that I will say.

So now to the acknowledgement. BIG shout out to my alpha reader Debi, who I swear is the best person EVER. She catches things that no one else does. I adore her immensely, and quite frankly I don't think I would've made it without her these last few months. She's been my steady rock. My confident and my best friend. Something that I don't put lightly. She's seen me through some dark times, and I'm forever grateful for her words when I lost Lani a few weeks ago.

Secondly, I have to thank Tammi for letting me know it was okay to write about Scotland. She was my #TravelMate throughout the country. We both fell in love. Thank you for reading their story and loving it. To my OGB and S-Gals crew. All I can say is thank you for letting me be who I am. Y'all make me a better person. I'm so glad I have each and every single one of you in my life. Love you all!

Stevie, thank you for being such a good friend to me. I don't think we go a day without talking generally, but beyond the normal book talk. Thank you for always being an understanding ear and checking on me. #Squirrel-AndAlien

Big shout out to my editor Jenn (aka J Woo). Gahhhh I love you so much. Thank you for loving their story. I won't lie, it made me nervous writing this story knowing you were going to be reading it. Thank you for making sure my Scottish brogue sounded right, because half the time I forgot that their accents do sound like that. I can't wait to share Scotland with you next year!!!

I know I will miss someone but again thank you for the readers and bloggers for taking their time out to read this story and for leaving your review.
Sláinte Mhaith

ABOUT THE *author*

J. Lum resides in the Northern Virginia area. While she calls Virginia home, she is constantly on the go. She's got a constant case of #Wanderlust; most of the time, you can find her traveling around the world to see her book besties or checking off her bucket list places. Her second home away from home is Hawaii, where her family is from. The love for the ocean runs through her veins. She also has a love of ALL pugs, unicorns, and anything chocolate. She and coffee have been having a love affair for many years.

FOR MORE INFORMATION:

http://www.authorjlum.com

BOOK+MAIN—@JLUM

facebook.com/authorjlum

twitter.com/authorjlum

instagram.com/authorjlum

amazon.com/author/jlum

9 780999 142356